THE COMMUTERS

JANE SANDERS

℞

Bookworm of Retford

First published 2014
Bookworm of Retford
1 Spa Lane, Retford Notts. DN22 6EA
www.bookwormretford.co.uk

ISBN 978-0992785-727

A catalogue record of this book is available from the British
Library.

Cover illustration by Katie Meads

The Commuters

Jane Sanders is a solicitor and has been commuting for most of her working life from a peaceful market town to the city. Her long, twice-daily journey has been an ideal time to write this, her first novel.

Author's Note

This is a work of fiction.
All characters in this book are imaginary and names
and situations used are of my own invention. Any
resemblance to real persons living or dead or train
companies and their employees is coincidental.

Chapters

Prologue

It would be so easy. Just a step off the platform. Guaranteed. Finished. Problems solved. He was the dependable type, always someone to sort everything out. No problem too great. But no-one had suspected that he had problems. Everyone - friends, family and work colleagues - took it for granted that he was in control. He was; and in that controlled manner he solved the biggest problem of all.

Here we go again

"Morning, morning. Late again," he said to no one in particular. Anthony looked up at the platform clock, wondering why the train could not, for once, be on time. Every minute late meant problems on the Tube, a crush of people to wade through, and late into the office.

Anthony liked to be organised. He needed to be in the office at 8.50 am precisely; this gave him ten minutes before the majority of his 'team' arrived. Those ten minutes were vital to his day. He didn't understand the need to call en route for a take-away coffee, to be carried hot and spilling across the office block main entrance, into the lift and onto their floor. By the time they arrived, with burnt fingers covered in sickly coffee, surely the thrill of a drink had vanished. Anthony often wondered why they couldn't just use the office kettle.

The office was Anthony's life. He had arrived, as expected, as a young graduate following in his father's footsteps. No other career had been considered by anyone. He had progressed well and passed all the necessary exams with distinction. A good family trait and tradition. Very considerately, according to his father, he had married the senior partner's daughter and in good time became the father of a boy and a girl, thereby ensuring longevity and progress of the firm. His wife naturally did not have paid employment, but worked tirelessly promoting her chosen charities and, of course, arranging their social life.

"Morning, Anthony," said Simon as they stood at the precise spot on the platform where they knew from years of experience the door to coach F of the train would open. When, of course, it chose to arrive. "Good day ahead?"

" Same as ever, Simon," replied Anthony. "Same as ever."

Simon was always jovial, no matter what time of day it was. Of course, he was at least twenty-five years younger than Anthony, and consequently had not been commuting for as long. Life was exciting for him. He had a young wife, who had a good career locally, and two young children in the nearby prep school. The longer hours at the school meant that both of them could do a full day's work and his wife could pick the children up after their school clubs. Simon was always bubbling about his job and the future.

"Off to Hong Kong again next week," Simon told Anthony. "The office there seems incapable of managing without me. Luckily I can take Lucy with me this time. She's managed to get a few days off work and her parents are having the children. We can't wait. Good chance to enjoy a good hotel on expenses and search out some new restaurants. You ought to give it a go, Anthony. You'd enjoy it."

Anthony preferred his annual trip to Cornwall and did not understand this fad of people always wanting to jet around the world. Secretly, he found Simon a bit over the top, and usually couldn't wait to get on the train so that he could sit in his usual place and open his newspaper. Then there would be no reason to talk.

And still the train did not arrive. Over the loudspeaker the least offensive of the platform staff announced the delay of ten minutes due to "signalling failure". Number three on their list of excuses. At least this particular member of staff usually tried to sound hopeful. If it had been one of the others, the excuse would have been relayed in a bored monotone.

Gerry, with his collapsible bike, then suddenly arrived, as usual out of breath and red in the face. "Good job it's late otherwise I would have missed it," he said as he tried to collapse his bike into the size of one tyre. He said this most mornings, of course, as he was always last- minute. The beads of sweat were now beginning to drip from under his cycle helmet. When he took off his helmet his curly red hair stuck to his head. Not that it mattered to Gerry. He was like this every morning. He simply put his hand through his hair and then used the same hand to wipe his brow.

Anthony often wondered how anyone could start a working day like this. Perhaps, he thought kindly, Gerry had a shower at work when he arrived, and appeared through his office door as a suave and debonair businessman, smelling of shampoo and cologne. He suspected, however, that that would not be the case. Gerry was some sort of rail network employee and probably had his hands full of grease all day. Fortunately for Anthony, Gerry chose always to sit in a corner seat each morning on his own and plug in his earphones.

Anthony wondered about earphones and how they managed to stay in the ears. On the very few occasions when he had tried to listen to Radio Four on his small travel radio his earphones would not stay in. They kept jumping out and falling on the table or the seat next to him, picking up innumerable germs. They made his ears hurt as well, and so the whole experiment was discarded.

No, he preferred to read his newspaper in peace. That way he could keep up to date with what was happening in the world, and didn't have to speak to anyone. He preferred it that way and was always pleased when Simon got out his laptop. He spent the entire journey on the laptop. Perhaps he was on the Internet reading the news, perhaps he was working, or perhaps he watched films. Anthony never asked.

At least Simon always looked smart and tidy. In fact, he always looked scrubbed and fresh and eager. Had, Anthony thought, he himself ever looked like that? He envied Simon's optimism. Everything seemed to go right for Simon, securing that plum job, finding that cheap mortgage to buy the house with the swimming pool, pretty wife and two perfect children.

Anthony thought briefly about his own children. Neither, it had turned out, had the least interest in becoming lawyers, let alone going into the firm. The last time he had heard from his son he was backpacking around Thailand with no desire to come home and get a proper job. His daughter was no better. She was living with some undesirable man and a group of alternative life-stylers on benefits. Anthony shuddered. He was pleased his father had not lived to see them in their chosen lives. He would have blamed Anthony.

In the distance the train could be seen approaching, and at that very moment Eleanor appeared on cue, looking elegant, confident and classy. "How do you manage it? Every day you walk on to the platform at exactly the right time," said Simon. "One of these days, you know, you'll miss it."

"I haven't yet," said Eleanor softly, "and I don't think I ever will. I can see the train coming from my bedroom window and I know how long precisely it takes me to get here from my house."

Anthony liked that about Eleanor. She was in control and neat and tidy and organised. She was friendly but in a calm, quiet manner. She spoke to everyone if they talked to her but was also, it appeared, more than happy to speak to no one, sit in her usual seat on the train and read her paper or work. It made him feel warm and at peace.

Since the train was running late, the guard was eager to get everyone on quickly. The guard always dreaded this, as he knew from years of experience that the collapsible bike would cause trouble. Why, he wondered, did people have to mess up his trains with such contraptions? They refused to be parted from them and put them in the guard's van. No, they insisted on putting them in the 'reserved for luggage' sections. But the guard felt that they were not luggage: they were dirty, oily bits of steel and should know their place - in the guard's van.

Gerry struggled his way on to the train, being careful not to get too close to Eleanor's black suit and sheer stockings. It had happened once, causing an ugly black grease-mark around the hem of her skirt and onto her legs. The look she gave him made him realise that it was not going to happen again. He had never had much success with women of any kind. After an unsuccessful marriage he now lived alone and preferred it that way: no one to moan at him or complain about his bicycle.

It had been a difficult start for Simon that day. He was used to the early mornings and was content to put up with the commute for the sake of his career. But his youngest child had been sick in the night and he had spent most of the time with him in the bathroom. His wife needed her sleep, he thought. He didn't know how she managed to work full-time and sort out the children. But he was proud of his achievements and readily accepted difficulties along the way. He relished the time on the train: a period of peace and quiet when he could prepare himself for his day and what he was going to do. He loved his job. He had started out in the clothing manufacturing company as the office boy, doing the post and running errands. He had never really liked school and had left with the basic GCSE passes. But he had ambition.

His father had told him he could have what he wanted if he stuck at things and aimed high. "Go for it and be the boss. Don't accept anything less. You choose the lifestyle you want and make sure you get it. "Aim for the top," he would say. Simon grew up believing he could be the Prime Minister if he chose. He loved the way his father had always had faith in him to make his lifestyle and stick to it. "Book learning is overrated," he would say. "What you need is practical experience. That's what will get you on."

So Simon had got a job in a clothing manufacturing company: good, solid option but with opportunities to advance. Simon knew he could succeed. He just needed to keep at it and work hard and he would do it. Fortunately for him the Managing Director took a shine to him: always punctual and thorough. The MD saw potential in him. Whenever the MD wanted anything Simon was always there, whether it was coffee, post, statistics or information as to what the current office gossip was. Simon got to know everything. He was very popular. Everyone trusted him to be there and do whatever was asked of him. Slowly and subtly Simon gained the confidence of everyone, and slowly and surely he climbed the company ladder.

The MD thought he was wasted in the post-room and appointed him to the role of 'trainee'. In this role Simon flourished. He was looked after, as no one regarded him as a threat. He had spent years in that role as trainee, learning as much as he could from every member of staff. His patience and hard work eventually and quietly resulted in promotions, until he was given the Far East desk. This was a position he had spent twenty years dreaming about. It also enabled him to hold on to that final dream. As his father had said, he should aim high. He could be the MD and would be the MD. But all in good time, subtly and quietly. You see, it was 'just Simon from the post-room'. No-one questioned how he had arrived at his current post, because everyone liked him and no-one noticed how, over the years, he had been progressing.

He arrived at the station, tired but as eager as ever to get to work. The drive to the station had been difficult. He had got caught behind a tractor. Of course, he always allowed three minutes for any such event, but he knew that if he didn't get to the station by 5.45 he would have difficulty parking in his usual place. He managed happily to pull into the parking slot at 5.46. Ah, he thought to himself, managed to make up the time. He was pleased with himself. He checked in his mirror to make sure his hair was OK and he hadn't left any stubble around his face after shaving, and quickly got out of his car. He was glad he had bought the 4x4. It was really too big for Lucy, but was wonderful for driving along country lanes early in the mornings. He let Lucy have the little sports car. It suited her. He did accept, though, that when the children were bigger they would have to do a swap.

He walked onto the platform. First there again, he thought. Time to collect myself. Then he spotted Anthony appearing in his vague and tired way. He worried about Anthony. He looked tired and depressed. Perhaps, Simon thought, he had had enough of commuting and should retire. Simon thought the fire had gone out of him, if, that is, there ever was any fire. Simon somehow doubted it. Every morning Simon tried to cheer him up, to suggest things to do or places to visit. But Anthony never appeared interested. Simon knew he had done the journey for years, and that he himself had only been commuting for a couple of years, since he had managed to buy his wonderful dream home in a little village. Anthony has no plan or purpose in life, he thought. That's his problem. He didn't even seem to be keen on holidays.

"Have you decided where you are going on holiday this year, Anthony?" he asked.

"Oh," said Anthony, "Cornwall again. We like it there. It's comforting to know what to expect and frankly we don't fancy the idea of going abroad. We did try a cruise once but never again. Hideous people, Simon. Have you ever been on one?"

"No," replied Simon. "I don't think we're quite ready for them. Too restricting for the children and we prefer discovering places for ourselves."

Both Simon and Anthony then spotted Gerry arriving with his bike. It always amused Simon the way Gerry seemed to be surgically attached to his bike. Simon liked exercise, but in its correct place: a lunchtime run followed by a shower at work. It made him ready for the afternoon, reinvigorated and alert. But cycling to the station at 5.30 in the morning seemed to him madness, and then to cycle through the London traffic was foolhardy. Had Gerry not read the statistics of injury and death to cyclists in London? Certainly, Simon could not consider sitting on a train for an hour, sweaty and uncomfortable. 'A tidy body means a tidy mind' had been his father's motto, and

Simon had always believed that this was a good approach to life.

"Good cycle in, Gerry? " Simon enquired.

"Yes, fine, thanks," he replied. Gerry never really liked talking to anyone. He preferred his own company. He felt secure with himself: no one to hassle him and no one to make him feel inadequate. He had learned over the years that he would always fail to create a good impression with everyone and so now he never bothered to try. He acknowledged that he would always fail in any event. No, he was happier when he knew that no one was expecting anything from him. He preferred it that way. It hadn't always been so.

During his married life he had felt relatively happy. The children had come along and he thought that his life was fine. He had failed to see what his wife's view of life was, however. The divorce had hit him badly. He had felt rejected and alone. But he had grown to accept these feelings and now he actively chose to be on his own. Safer that way, he thought. No one to upset him again. No need to try to impress. He was done with that life. He kept himself to himself and positively enjoyed his solitude and his timetables. His job in the railways sorting out the timetables and planning times on all the national routes was a job made for him. He liked the neatness of the timetables, how everything fitted together and was organised. He enjoyed the annual timetable changes, and thought of them as puzzles waiting to be solved. New lines and new trains made him feel happy. He could immerse himself in them and they didn't complain to him. As long as he filed them all in time he was left alone.

Eleanor appeared on time, looking perfect as always. Simon admitted to himself that he felt a little intimidated by Eleanor. She was always friendly enough, but you could never actually work out what she was thinking. She just looked so calm all the time. She was older, of course, and had been doing this journey for years. But it was hard to work out exactly how old she was. She was a runner, he knew, and therefore was a woman who looked after herself. They often talked about running, marathons and 10Ks and training. But Simon knew that she was a weekend runner only. He could not imagine her with dishevelled hair and running kit.

"Off to Hong Kong next week," he said to her as they got on the train.

"Brilliant!" she replied. "I've been there several times and it's excellent. I went there last year on the way back from Australia. Is it business or pleasure?" she asked, genuinely interested.

"A bit of both," he said. "Lucy is coming with me. A trip without the kids."

"Excellent, just what you need," she replied. "I remember when I used to get trips abroad with my job years ago. Always good fun provided you could bring something positive to report back to the office and justify the price," she joked.

She then sat down in her normal seat and opened her briefcase. Pulling out a file and taking out her fountain pen from her handbag, she began to work. This was her life. She was married to the job. She had always given all her life to it. She lived alone and always had done since she had started work. She had stayed in her hometown, choosing to commute to work rather than get a local job. She was ambitious and had wanted to succeed in the bank from a young age when she had first started to visit the bank with her father to deposit her pocket money. She was fascinated with collecting money and making it work. She liked to see it grow in an account and imagined what she could do with it. She now advised customers what to do with their savings and helped them plan for their futures and lives. She had been promoted to commercial banking in a large branch in the city. It was a good opportunity to be at the coalface, and see how all the schemes and policies could work in practice. She had found it tough at first to go back into a local branch but accepted the potential. She knew it was a test of her ability and that the bank was hoping to use her as an example of their policies. So she had been working even harder to show them that she could succeed. She didn't have anything else in her life apart from this, and she had to make it work.

Simon opened up his computer and logged on to his office site. After dealing with his e-mails and tweaking the report which needed to be ready for the 9 o'clock meeting, he began to Google restaurants in Hong Kong and investigate the people he was going to meet over there. One step ahead, he thought to himself. Always necessary to be prepared.

The train glided along, already late and incapable of trying to make up time. Stops along the way resulted in more and more commuters filing in one by one, eagerly trying to sit down in their usual seats and looking annoyed if a day traveller had had the audacity to sit in it. There was always a disturbance for at least five minutes until they had all had their obligatory chat and settled down to their individual routines. Film watchers on their laptops, music listeners on their iPods, readers, newspaper guzzlers, sleepers, commuters worried about the day ahead, planners with work set out on their laptops, graph readers and starers-into-space - all accepted the unavoidable journey into work, all held captive by the railway company for a brief (and sometimes not-so-brief) period of time. The excuse for the delay this time was 'signal failure', but by the third stop it was clear that it had become 'theft of lead', and then 'a build-up of trains into the capital'. Not a good day. All we need now, thought the commuters, was 'an obstacle on the track' – a euphemism for a suicide. This would mean a delay of at least an hour, an hour no one wanted to spend on the train. The train pulled into the station exactly twenty-nine minutes late - not long enough to claim compensation, which kicked in at thirty minutes.

Everyone filed out in an orderly manner with a resigned look on their faces. Here we go again, they all thought. Another day. They each breathed in the oxygen of the city to provide them with the rush of adrenalin necessary to fight the crowds and start the day, negotiate the Tube, walk to the office or catch the bus. Each minute brought a heightened awareness of the requirements of the day ahead and gradually everyone rose to the occasion. Once they were outside the station, the sounds impacted upon each of them as if by surprise. But this happened every day: from the quiet and peace of the train to the vibrant sounds of the city. Brakes squealing, sirens going, buses passing, crowds of people merging together waiting at traffic lights, cyclists skipping them at speed and shouts from angry pedestrians. Everyone busy to get somewhere and be somewhere else. No one smiled. No one spoke. Everyone an island.

Anthony, Simon, Gerry and Eleanor stepped off the train independently from each other and without talking. They were transformed into work mode, a survival technique necessary to deal with the day. "See you this evening," was all they could muster.

Anthony

Anthony had been a qualified solicitor from the age of twenty-four. His parents had not expected anything else from him. His father had built up the practice shortly after the war and, with hard work and determination, had succeeded in developing a respected medium-sized firm in the city. Their clients were mostly city-established people, used to being able to pop in or pick up the phone at a moment's notice and get help and advice. His father had had a good reputation based upon thoroughness and honesty. He had belonged to the right clubs and slowly a loyal following was attracted. Into this environment Anthony had arrived straight from Law School and been given a solid fundamental training in the law. He had decided to follow Litigation, which at the time seemed more exciting than Conveyancing and has the added advantage that he didn't have to see his father in the office very much, since it meant that he would often be in court.

So Anthony had slotted in without having to think or make a choice. He learnt to draft documents and appear in court, and for a while he might have said that he was happy with his job and his life. Marrying the daughter of his father's partner in the firm had seemed at the time the most sensible path. He hadn't really had much success with women and it just seemed the easiest route. Certainly it was a popular decision within the office. Neat and tidy, and Anthony liked neatness and control and everything in order.

But over the years changes in law and practice had transformed the office. Computers had taken over from the typewriter and accounts were no longer a ledger card for each client, but needed a whole computerised system themselves. Regulations imposed by the Law Society had further increased his worries. It seemed necessary to do so much more than just the work. Anthony had found it difficult to come to terms with these changes. Now it appeared most firms were writing to each other by e-mail. Even the courts expected you to send orders and letters to them by e-mail direct to the judge. In some cases the solicitor or barrister acting for the other side brought a very clever gadget upon which they could type up orders there and then and e-mail them in court to the judge in court. Anthony could not get his head around this. He liked time to consider orders and documents, and advise his clients after this consideration, not in the rush of the hearing day when they had been in court for hours.

Anthony used his secretary to do all his letters and typing, and positively refused to write his own e-mails. But he realised that eventually this would have to change.

Anthony arrived in his office, and because the train had been half an hour late a number of people had already arrived. "Hello, Anthony," said one of his junior partners. "Trouble on the train?"

"Yes," he replied. "There's always one excuse or another. They just make it up as they go along. I don't believe a word they say. They have a list of excuses."

"You want to live in town," the young partner replied. "I've just moved into a great flat overlooking the river. Bit pricey but worth it. Brilliant views and we can go out without the worry of the last train home. You ought to move. Give you a new lease of life. Oh, by the way, I've opened the post already. Yours is on your chair."

"Thank you. Well done," replied Anthony. Anthony was annoyed. He always liked to open the post. He felt it to be one of the last remaining roles of the senior partner. But he acknowledged that there was little post these days. Most came by that darned e-mail. Even faxes were becoming obsolete.

He walked into his room and sat down, turning on his computer and picking up his post from the chair. Very little of interest: an invite to a cocktail party, adverts from bailiffs offering their services and a letter unopened from the landlords of his office building. He knew the lease was coming to an end and that he would have to negotiate new terms. He had a meeting with the bank this morning and would try to persuade them to extend the overdraft yet again.

He logged on to his computer, an action which always made him angry. He still could not understand why everything had to be dominated by this machine. Gone were normal letters and notes, ledgers and paper trails. Instead, everything had to be on this screen. Of course, as he had always known, the darned thing was forever breaking down or freezing or items became hidden. So he had been persuaded to employ people to sort out these messes. More expense. A group of people, the IT department, with geeks who seemed to work magic from the end of a phone. He was often left wondering how someone could take control of his computer screen from somewhere else. The little arrow, the cursor as he was told to call it, moving around the screen as if it had a life of its own. Clicking here and there, fixing whatever problem arose. Colin in IT always seemed to know the answer but his expertise came at a price. Anthony was told that it was necessary by one of his partners, but he still did not understand why Colin needed two assistants to do his job. But he supposed they always seemed busy, fixing, adapting, inputting new forms, updates and everything that frankly made Anthony feel a bit queasy.

At least Anthony had managed to keep hold of his secretary, who faithfully brought him his cup of coffee and two chocolate digestives at 11.00 sharp. As part of the cost-cutting exercises, most of the other members of the firm had lost their secretaries and had been told to do their own work straight onto the computer. Anthony had been told that this was the way forward and the only way to go. Whilst he accepted the much-needed reduction in staffing costs he did question whether in fact everyone else was spending their time wisely, and half- suspected that they could get more actual work done if they dictated letters to a secretary like in the old days. The time spent on typing and drafting documents, letters and e-mails, Anthony believed, could more usefully and profitably be spent on doing what they were trained to do - the law.

"Morning, Mr Simpson. Bit late this morning, aren't you? Don't forget your appointment at 10.00 at the bank. I've printed off everything you'll need from the computer. All you have to do is print off office bank account details when they are up to date. Everything else is there. Quite a lot of paperwork, I'm afraid. Took me ages to print it all off. Good job my printer was working properly today. Is there anything you would like me to do before you set off?"

His secretary spoke to him kindly at all times. She sat down on the chair opposite his desk with her notepad on her lap. Anthony liked his secretary. She had been with him almost as long as he could remember. She had started working for him when she was about eighteen years old, when he himself had first joined the firm. They had stayed together ever since, each one supporting the other in a restrained, but dignified, manner. Somehow she had managed to steer him through some tight spots along the way, and yet neither knew the other's life outside the office. Anthony liked it that way. He had striven to ensure against familiarity. But he had to admit he had become used to leaning upon her for support.

Surprisingly, she had realised in the early days that it would become necessary to master this computer thing. Fortunately, she had gone to college outside office hours and got herself some useful knowledge. Only in this way had Anthony been able to cope with technology, He basically left it all to her. She had shown him how to turn the dreadful thing on and look at his e-mails. But he did insist on dictating his replies to the e-mails to her so that she could do a proper letter in reply. She knew how to get into all the client information, something which totally baffled Anthony. The only matters which she did not touch were the accounts and banking details. The IT department had shown Anthony how to get into this information. He nostalgically thought back to ledger cards and bank statements, but had to accept that now all of this information was stored inside the computer, and the only way to get at it was through the machine.

Anthony knew the meeting with the bank was going to be difficult, and so, after a few brief dictations to his secretary, he would get all the accounts information out of his computer and peruse it before the meeting. One of his partners was going to go to the bank with him. He trusted his partner, Nicholas. Younger than him but still in tune with his way of thinking, unlike the others who seemed to view matters from an entirely different perspective. Nicholas was old enough to remember what it used to be like in the office, when everyone had his own secretary and everyone stopped for a mid-morning coffee break. Now, everyone seemed to want coffee in cardboard cups throughout the day. He stuck to his cup and saucer and acknowledged he was lucky to have someone to make him coffee in the morning and tea in the afternoon.

They walked out of the office into the street: taxis and buses and bicycles and people, all fighting to get somewhere. Everyone always in a hurry. It was raining, as ever, and Anthony carefully took out of his briefcase his collapsible umbrella. Nicholas didn't have one, so he pulled up his collar on his Mac.

"When will this rain stop?" he asked Anthony. "It seems to have been raining for months. Why do we put up with it, Anthony? As soon as I can I want to finish and move abroad, somewhere in the sun. When are *you* going to finish?"

"I haven't really thought about it," Anthony replied. "I don't know what I would do. I don't like the heat and can't think of anything worse than getting hot and sticky under a continental sun. I quite like the rain."

It suited his character, thought Nicholas, but didn't say so. He had learnt over the years to keep a lot of his thoughts to himself in the office. He had for months been checking the accounts and he was rather anxious about this meeting with the bank. He didn't seem to understand why they were not making as much money as before. He knew everyone was feeling the downturn in the economy, and certainly the number of new clients had slowed down. In fact, even some of the older and loyal clients didn't seem to get in touch as much. The partners had tried all sorts of new methods to change their working practices and become more efficient, but it hadn't made much difference. Still, Nicholas didn't worry too much. He was already thinking of that little place in the sun and planned to get there as soon as he could.

Anthony was confident as he strode into the bank. He had always liked the building: a proper building, not one of those new modern glass-and-steel affairs. It had high ceilings and cornices, dark woodwork and old-fashioned counters. He admitted that the glass partitions at the counters didn't seem to fit in, though, and assumed the bank had had to accept heightened security. He had dealt with the same bank manager for years. He knew their firm inside out. He had been looking after them for as long as Anthony could remember. Anthony prided himself that this close personal relationship always worked to the firm's advantage and didn't begrudge the fine bottle of wine he sent over to the manager every Christmas. He regarded their relationship as civilised and one of the few remaining decent aspects of professional life in the City.

Anthony and Nicholas entered through the heavy swivel doors and walked straight up to the manager's office. They were greeted by a young girl. She seemed new. She had on a smart bank-issue suit and a short scarf tied around her neck. Her hair was blonde and straight and looked as if it had been ironed.

"Hello," she said. "You must be Mr Simpson and Mr Pargeter from Simpson and Sons?"

"Yes, that's correct, Miss. The Manager is expecting us," Anthony replied.

"Your appointment today is with Ms Grant, the Customer Relations Manager. She will be with you shortly," the young girl said.

"No," said Anthony, "you're mistaken, Miss. We are here to see Mr Hughes, the Manager, as usual, for our monthly meeting. Kindly tell him we've arrived."

The young girl looked directly at Anthony and said, "I'm sorry, Mr Simpson, but Mr Hughes is no longer with the bank. He's retired and his position has now been taken by Ms Grant. Please take a seat."

With that, the young straight-haired girl disappeared, and Anthony and Nicholas were left looking around for a seat. Anthony became flustered. Why, he asked himself, hadn't Mr Hughes forewarned him of this? What had happened to him? Anthony was rather annoyed that after all these years he had not been given the courtesy of a letter or phone call from the bank or Mr Hughes.

"Rum thing this, eh, Nicholas? What do you think?"

"Oh," replied Nicholas, "it's happening all over. My own local bank hasn't had a manager for years now. No-one knows you anymore. But I think the majority of folk do their banking online these days and the banks have had to adapt."

Anthony looked appalled. "Well, I don't do my banking online," he said, "and have no intention of doing so. I must admit I leave it all to my wife to go into the local branch. She may have noticed a change but hasn't mentioned it."

Anthony was unsure as to how to deal with Ms Grant. He assumed she would have no knowledge of his firm or the accounts. No doubt he would have to guide her through them and then explain why they needed to extend their overdraft facility again. It had always been a mere formality before, as Mr Hughes had seen all the ups and downs over the years.

Anthony looked up and saw a young woman striding purposefully towards them. She also was wearing a bank-issue suit and a scarf around her neck. She had long, brown hair falling over her shoulders and very high-heeled shoes. The suit seemed to fit her tightly, showing off her clearly honed and fit figure. Her strong black glasses emphasised her eyes, which, Anthony could see, were heavily made up with eyeliner and mascara. As she approached, Anthony wondered why all young girls these days seemed to look the same. When, he wondered, had they started to infiltrate the business world? Perhaps that was the reason why everything seemed to be changing. He started to feel depressed.

"Good morning, Mr Simpson and Mr Pargeter," she said. "I'm so sorry for keeping you waiting. I'm Tracey Grant, your Customer Relations Manager. Do follow me." She led them into Mr Hughes's old room. "Do take a seat. Can I offer you some coffee?"

A tray with tea and coffee and mugs was on the side table with a plate of biscuits and milk and sugar. The table was new, glass with a steel surround. Anthony started to feel uncomfortable. He looked around the room. What had happened to it? Where was Mr Hughes's old desk, the large mahogany one with green baize leather top and leather chairs? He had been asked to sit on some peculiar steel chairs with a cushion which seemed to dip down, making him feel lower than normal. The desk was glass with steel legs and there was only a computer on it. Where were all the papers, the in/out tray, pens, piles of files and all the usual items which surely most people had on their desks and certainly Mr Hughes had had?

"We're here to talk about your banking arrangements, I understand, with particular reference to your overdraft facility. Is this correct?" Ms Grant asked forcefully, looking at them directly through her dark-rimmed glasses. Anthony noticed as she touched her glasses that her fingernails were painted red. But not only red - they had some sort of pattern on them. He had noticed this on some of the young typists at the office and wondered at this new craze. He found it difficult to accept, however, such nails on a person who was about to make a fundamental decision as to his firm's future.

"I think there's been some mistake," he replied. "I usually see Mr Hughes, who has been looking after our firm for over twenty years. All the details will be in our file somewhere and he must have left some notes in it for your assistance. Perhaps you would like to look at them so that our conversation could be more constructive, and they might enable you to understand what exactly we do." Anthony spoke somewhat haughtily. He didn't like this girl and certainly did not want to trust his firm's future with her.

"Well, Mr Simpson," she said, "I'm grateful for your concern. However, everything is on my computer. I am at the moment looking at the situation of both your office account and client account and have in front of me the history over a significant number of years. Mr Hughes has now retired, and I have been appointed to look after all the accounts he ran. I do this in conjunction with our Area Manager, Mr Forsyte, who oversees everything. I have, of course, discussed matters with him before you arrived. Unfortunately, we are both very concerned at the history of your office account. I see that for the last twelve months the number of your monthly invoices has been reducing and your gross profits have significantly deteriorated. Your outstanding bills have risen and your work in progress appears to accumulate and not be picked up in your invoicing each month in total. Conversely, your outgoings have increased. Your rent is significantly higher and will increase further, following your pending rent review. Your wages bill is greater than it has ever been. Are you following me?"

Anthony looked at her in disbelief. She was talking like a robot. What had happened to the friendly chat over lunch and a good bottle of Burgundy?

"Look, Miss," he replied, "I really am not prepared to discuss this with you. You have only just looked into my firm. It has been going for over sixty years. I am the second generation of Simpsons, and Mr Hughes, I felt, was one of the family." He looked across to Nicholas, who was just sitting there staring at the girl, clearly taken in by her position and looks. "What do you think, Nicholas?" he asked loudly.

"Well," said Nicholas, "I'm sure Ms Grant has everything on her computer, and after all the figures cannot be disputed."

"That's not the point," said Anthony, who was now becoming rather annoyed. He could feel himself flushing in the face. The heat had started in his feet and had gradually been moving up his body from the moment he had been told that Mr Hughes had retired. He felt he was going to explode. He knew that shouting would do no good, neither would arguing. However, something had to be done. He tried to calm himself down and call upon all the resources of his training and experience.

"Miss Grant, you mentioned that you work with an Area Manager, a Mr Forsyte I think you said. Kindly make arrangements for us to see him as soon as possible," said Anthony, buying time so that he could work out a strategy.

"Actually," she replied, "he's at this bank this afternoon. Shall we say 4.30 back here, gentlemen? I shall look forward to it." With that, she stood up, shook hands with Anthony and Nicholas and was gone, back into the inner sanctum of the bank, leaving Anthony and Nicholas standing in Mr Hughes's old room.

"So what now, Anthony?" asked Nicholas as they walked out of the bank. "We know what the figures are like. We can't afford to fall out with the bank. We need them. The staff needs them. Personally, I thought she looked quite professional."

"Professional?" enquired Anthony. "You call that professional, with her painted nails and her funny hair and nothing on the desk? No, believe me Nicholas, when we talk to the man in charge this afternoon everything will be OK," he added, confidently.

They walked quickly and quietly back to the office with no further conversation, each of them with his own thoughts and fears. Nicholas could see the worst-case scenario, but kept in mind his place in the sun. Anthony, however, was frightened. He felt exposed without Mr Hughes. For years they had had a good relationship, one of mutual support. In lean years the bank had kept the firm going and in the good years the bank appreciated the loyalty of the firm to the bank. Swings and roundabouts. But now Anthony was scared. He didn't have a game plan and had not been given time to construct one. He liked to plan and to be ready. Ms Grant had taken him off-guard. The unexpected and unnerving. But he couldn't let Nicholas see his fear. No. Nicholas looked up to him.

Always had done. Anthony appreciated this, but this time he did not know how he was going to be able to come out of this one with any credibility.

So, later in the day, Nicholas and Anthony walked once again to the bank, Anthony now confident that all would be well. He had spent his lunchtime going over the figures and the recent partners' meeting notes, when they had discussed cost-cuttings and marketing strategies. Anthony had not really participated fully in the meeting, but he now read eagerly the Minutes and digested the arguments.

Nicholas was a little anxious. "Look, Anthony," he said, "I've printed off all the schedules I could think of, all the bank statements and summaries, aged debt reports and work-in-progress reports. I have got an up-to-date printout of each fee earner's past month's work, and what we will be billing this month. I have a report from Accounts on the current debts and what the position is on follow-up and suing the clients. I have done comparisons and targets month-on-month, year-on-year. I hope it's enough."

"Of course it'll be enough, Nicholas. Stop worrying. I've had numerous meetings like this over the years with old Hughes. A good Burgundy usually did the trick," Anthony replied.

"But look, Anthony," said Nicholas, "it isn't like that anymore. You heard what Ms Grant said. She had everything there on her computer. Have you thought what we are going to do if they don't extend our overdraft? I think we should have some plans. Some fall-back position."

"And what fall-back position could that possibly be, Nicholas?" Anthony enquired. "We've already given them charges on our properties. We don't own our office and I doubt if we could make any further cutbacks to staff or indeed our wages bill. No, it'll be fine. Leave it to me," he said, smiling.

With that, the pair walked slowly over to the bank. They didn't have to wait this time but were shown immediately into Mr Hughes's old room. This is more like it, thought Anthony. No doubt the Area Manager has got it all sorted now and explained to that young woman how to handle established customers.

"Do sit down, Mr Simpson and Mr Pargeter. My name is Steven Forsyte, the Area Manager," said Mr Forsyte quietly and calmly as everyone sat down. "You know Ms Grant, of course, from this morning. Can I offer you tea or coffee?"

"No, nothing, thank you," replied Anthony, wondering how on earth he could possibly drink tea sitting on these peculiar chairs, which felt as if they were going to collapse any minute and trap you, legs in the air. Anthony knew he had to keep his decorum, but was at last impressed that someone was now in control.

"Well," said Mr Forsyte, "I've reviewed your circumstances and looked at all the accounts and schedules. I assume you have put in place what we asked for on the last occasion?" he asked.

"Well," replied Nicholas, proffering all his own schedules and comparisons, "I've summarised our current position and, as you can see, although it doesn't look too rosy, we have tried to make ourselves leaner and fitter."

Nicholas thought that comment would cause a bit of a smile; instead, it caused a sneer from Mr Forsyte.

"Have the recommendations been put in place?" he asked.

"Well," replied Anthony, "not exactly. We have made some redundancies, those wanting to go, and some volunteered to reduce their working hours. We have therefore managed to make some savings," Anthony added confidently.

"But clearly," continued Mr Forsyte, "they haven't worked. You are asking the bank to take on your risk and I'm afraid, as far as I can see, you have not met us on any point on the five-point plan we put in place on the last occasion."

Anthony vaguely remembered a five-point plan being mentioned by Mr Hughes over the second bottle of Burgundy. All very tedious, he thought at the time, but agreed to it so that he could finish the lunch and get back to the office.

"Shall we go through each of the points in turn?" asked Mr Forsyte. Anthony and Nicholas looked at each other and feared the worse. "Aged debts," continued Mr Forsyte. "What has been done about these? There are significant monies owed to you. Have the plans been put into practice to chase these and collect the cash?"

"I believe so," replied Anthony.

"How exactly, Mr Simpson, have you addressed this?"

Anthony looked to Nicholas for assistance and was met with a blank face. "Our accounts team are dealing with it," responded Anthony.

"And how exactly are they dealing with it, Mr Simpson? To my mind they are clearly not doing a very good job. The aged debts have increased, not decreased," continued Mr Forsyte.

Again, Anthony was at a loss. He searched through all the printouts which Nicholas had handed to him: figures, all black figures on white paper. He had never understood these printouts. The old-fashioned ledger cards were so much easier. He fondly remembered Miss Drew, the Chief Accounts Clerk, who had looked after everything in his father's time and when he had been newly qualified. She had stayed with the firm all her life and retired at seventy years old. Anthony had never understood why she had to leave. She had no family. She had lasted only one year after this. Nothing left in her life. Now, although there was a team of six people inputting data onto the computer systems, Anthony felt he was no longer in control and struggled to understand what all the different papers actually meant.

"Work in progress," continued Mr Forsyte. "Clearly, the firm is struggling to find new sources of work or the staff are not recording time properly. Which is it, Mr Simpson?" he asked, his eyes piercing straight into Anthony's forehead.

Anthony had to acknowledge that work was not as plentiful as it had been. He had assumed it was the same for everyone. Other partners had brought in lawyers with supposed 'followings', but more often than not these followings did not materialise, and the firm had been left with a salary to pay but no income to pay it. Also, the firm had lost a couple of good clients, one a building company which itself had gone bust in the current economic climate and one an insurance company which had taken its work elsewhere where they had managed to negotiate a cheaper rate.

"Cut-backs and redundancies," Mr Forsyte continued, without giving Anthony time to come back to him on the previous point. "Can you explain to me how this has been implemented? I assume you have made an assessment following correct legal practices and reduced your workforce as far as possible?"

Anthony started to feel nauseous. He knew he had done no such thing. Yes, that young girl in Accounts had gone. She had been useless and couldn't even add up using a calculator. Yes, a couple of the girls had happily accepted shorter hours, but other than that the workforce remained the same. He knew that this would not be enough to satisfy the bank's five-point plan. But Anthony wondered how you could make people redundant when the job was their life, or they had a family to support, or they were old and not likely to get another job. Simpson and Sons had always been a family firm. It looked after everyone. He fondly remembered the days of cakes at birthdays and Christmas, half-day closing for the races and giving staff a sub when they were hard up.

"And finally," said Mr Forsyte, "long-term plan and strategy. Perhaps you would like to explain yours to me, Mr Simpson?" he enquired hopefully. Anthony remembered the last partners' meeting when they had discussed what they were going to do. He had been outvoted. Take more people on and expand, become totally computerised, do away with all the secretaries, merge with another firm of a similar ethos and background - these had been the plans, the strategy, irrespective of the cost, using funds from the bank overdraft facility, which not so many years ago the bank was falling over itself to give to them. A future based on quicksand, thought Anthony. None of the ideas had come to fruition. Despite some attempts to merge, no-one had wanted to form any sort of marriage with them. None of the fee-earners liked the idea of getting rid totally of all the secretaries and so one by one none of the ideas was implemented.

Anthony was unable to answer Mr Forsyte's questions, as there were no answers. No excuses. It had happened. The firm was in difficulties and dependent upon the bank to keep it going. He looked again at Nicholas, who was inexplicably on his mobile phone, either texting or receiving a text.

"I'm sorry, Mr Simpson," continued Mr Forsyte. "Until such time as the bank is satisfied that you have followed the five-point plan and everything is set up to secure a healthy and viable future, we cannot extend your overdraft and must demand repayment of our loan forthwith. Simpson and Sons is too great a risk for us. I see that we have our loans secured against the partners' houses, and we will commence proceedings to retrieve those loans in the absence of individual proposals which are acceptable to the bank. Good afternoon, gentlemen." With that, he left, followed by Ms Grant.

Anthony and Nicholas were left sitting in the room. The text on Nicholas's phone read "On way out". They got up and walked slowly towards the door.

"Call a partners' meeting tomorrow, nine o'clock, Nicholas, would you," Anthony said as he walked out of the bank. "I'm off home straightaway." With that, he was gone.

Simon

Simon marched off to the Tube with purpose. He knew it would take him fifteen minutes from the station to his office, provided the Tube was working properly. He looked the part. The new suit he had had made by the tailor in the East End fitted well and looked good. He had been recommended to him by a colleague at work, and the cost was well justified. Quality and hardwearing. It was necessary to look good in the clothing manufacturing industry. His company made clothes for the High Street chains, and it was Simon's job now to set up and oversee the factories abroad, which managed to make clothes at low prices to ensure good profitability here. Women's clothes mainly, and middle to low-end. Although Simon had no practical experience of manufacturing and no qualifications in business, he had been in the company head office for so long that he felt he knew how everything worked. Good, solid, practical experience, his father would say.

He sometimes wished he had stayed at school longer and got some qualifications, but he knew he had a business brain and quietly and subtly he had learned everything he knew from the people around him. He was proud that people trusted him and was always eager to prepare the reports for the board meetings.

As he walked from the Tube to the office, he thought about the board meeting today. He had prepared for it well. He enjoyed the walk from the Tube. It enabled him to collect his thoughts. He knew every shop in the street, every paving stone, all the bumps and uneven ones. He knew the crossings and the traffic lights and when it was safe to cross and when absolutely necessary to wait for the green man. At one crossing there were dozens of cyclists who all seemed to cross the junction together. Simon didn't know how you could arrive at work after a strenuous and dangerous ride in. He always thought it looked dangerous: the way they cycled in and out of the traffic, cutting in front of buses and vans. He also wondered at the women, many of whom seemed to cycle in high heels.

He arrived at his office and said good morning to the doorman. He always wore his security pass around his neck so that everyone knew he was meant to be there. It always seemed to him to be the most sensible approach. He had been told when he first started as the office boy that he should always wear it and so he did. He had never wanted to get into trouble. He liked procedure and protocols. They made him feel secure. Safe. Fitting in. He fitted into this company. A small cog in a big wheel but, he felt, a cog which was slowly and almost imperceptibly getting bigger and bigger. He relished the prospect of his trip to Hong Kong. He had been part of the team developing this outsourcing.

Manufacturing clothes in the UK had become too expensive. Very little profit could be made and he had helped in the research and planning of the production overseas. He had already had a couple of trips out to

Hong Kong, finding premises and staff and ensuring the work could be done within budget and in accordance with the standards required. The team had four members. Simon liked them all, but he had to admit they did make him feel a little uneasy. They all seemed so bright and innovative. They had all come into the company in the last couple of years, bringing their experience from competitors. They got on with Simon, but Simon couldn't help but feel that they were using him for his knowledge of the company and his relationships with everyone both senior and junior. He liked to help, though, and he quickly put aside all his uneasiness, explaining to himself that he was happy to help and, of course, they would have to rely on him. After all, he knew the company inside out. He knew the way things were done, who needed to be onside and kept informed, and who could help the most.

The planning and development of the Hong Kong site had been twelve months in the doing. It had to be run just like all the manufacturing plants in the UK, but more cheaply. Cheaper rents and cheaper wage bills meant that the product itself could be produced for half what it would cost in the UK. The individual items could be put out to retail at a price very much lower than their competitors'. Simon's role was to ensure uniformity and the transportation of the company ethos abroad.

He expected to have to go out there on a regular basis. He was already booked to go out next weekend and had been able to sneak in his wife for the trip. Some of the other team members had done this and the company had OK'd it, provided the job was done over there with minimum disruption. He looked forward to these trips. The project felt to Simon as a culmination of everything he had worked for all his life. He was competing on the big stage. His experience of the company was just as good, he felt, as these newcomers who seemed to have tons of qualifications but very little experience. He was able to show them how things were done. He had to admit to himself that he was surprised at how quickly they caught on and were able to move forward. He wondered where their confidence came from. Deep down he knew it was their education. Still, he put that to the back of his mind. He had to. It was something he didn't have. But, he reminded himself, he had the experience on the ground. Invaluable, he thought. Everyone liked him. He knew everyone and how everything worked.

Building himself up from the post-room, in and out of everyone's office, up and down each floor. Everyone liked his eagerness and smile. He talked to everyone and found out all there was to know about the company: who to get on with, who was important, and whom it was necessary not to fall out with. The small cog getting gradually bigger and bigger without anyone really noticing, apart from Simon himself.

"Morning, Mr Tomkinson," greeted the doorman. "Fine day today."

"Yes, it certainly is," replied Simon. He liked the doorman and the way he called him Mr Tomkinson. Respect and kindness. He liked that.

Simon moved toward the lift and was taken quickly to the tenth floor. Two floors off the top, he thought to himself. Getting there gradually. Starting in the basement and moving upwards. The best direction, he thought. He remembered the first floor and Mr Glastonbury in Accounts. Invoices and payments of accounts, credit control and ledgers - everything was computerised eventually, and he enjoyed how everything could be obtained just by tapping in an account number or name. A whole arena of figures past and present and projections for the future. Simon felt it was like the big picture: the company he knew but, on the big screen, coming into life, the real meaning of why they were all there - to make money.

He had enjoyed it in Accounts. People started to trust him there. He was thorough and careful and very soon they began to see the potential behind the smile.

Almost without anyone realising, he kept getting promoted: Design Section on the fourth floor, Production Section on the sixth floor, marketing on the eighth floor. It was here that he really did come into his own. He liked people and people liked him. He seemed to be able to entertain and be entertained and get orders. He was approachable and always available and always returned calls.

Of course, he had married exceptionally well. His wife was a great help to him. The clients loved her: very attractive and full of fun. She was always willing to get involved whenever necessary with dinners, cocktail parties and trips abroad. She was very glamorous but the clients thought perhaps high maintenance. They were wrong. She had a business head on her shoulders. She also knew what she was doing and had ambition. She worked in a local dress shop and seemed to have an endless supply of frocks. But her aim was to get all the necessary contacts and open up her own business in competition. She knew she could do it and was determined to follow through. A shop of her own would enable her to sort out the children as well.

It was Simon's time in the Marketing Department which had brought him into the realms of the twelfth floor and the Chief Executive of the company. He had started to attend meetings on a regular basis with the Head of Marketing, just to take notes at first and to produce necessary details about potential clients, which he always appeared to have at his fingertips. The Chief Executive, who had also come up through the ranks, began to notice how at every meeting they had Simon could supply the answer. It was for this reason that eventually, after twenty-five years at the company, Simon had been invited onto the Board. It seemed natural. He had arrived without anyone actually noticing the ascent. Of course, he wasn't invited into the inner core, not yet. He would not have expected that. But he was sitting at the table and there was only one other place he wanted to be: at the head.

The lift doors opened and he headed for his office.

"Hi, Simon," called one of the girls. "Norman wants to see you in his office. He told me to tell you as soon as you arrived."

"Thanks, Mel," Simon replied.

He was surprised that Norman wanted to meet him so early. Normally he arranged the regular meetings at the same time each Monday and the other necessary get-togethers a few days in advance. Simon tried to think what it could be. He couldn't think of any particular problems. The Hong Kong project was on target and as far as he was aware there had been no hitches. The other four members of the team had not flagged up anything to worry about.

He put his briefcase down by the side of his desk and logged on to his computer. He normally liked this time of day. He was usually one of the first to arrive on his floor. It gave him time to check his e-mails in peace, check his calendar and plan his day so that when everyone else arrived he was up and running - on top of everything. He had planned to write a summary of what he was going to be looking for on his next trip to Hong Kong, what he hoped to find, and identify any potential problems and to be ready with answers. Other members of the team had already prepared their own reports of the progress so far, and he had read all of them on his train journey in. He felt confident as to the progress of the project and his position within the planning.

His trip back to the lift and up to the twelfth floor therefore did not give him any anxiety; he was merely puzzled as to why Norman wanted to see him. The lift door opened and he walked towards Norman's PA. She was sitting behind a desk decorated with expensive lilies. This gave the feeling of peace and tranquillity. She ushered him into Norman's room. Simon entered and discovered that most of the other Board members were there, and his Hong Kong team. They were standing drinking coffee and looking concerned.

"Oh, hello, Simon. Here at last," Norman greeted Simon. "Sorry I didn't get a chance to give you a heads-up about this meeting. We only discovered last night that we would have to have to get together."

"What's it all about, Norman?" replied Simon, starting to look concerned.

"We have an important announcement to make, Simon. Gather round," Norman said cheerily.

Simon looked around the room. Everyone was there: his team, standing together as if in talks themselves; the inner core of the Board also huddled together, the remaining Board members looking as confused as Simon.

"Shall we all take a seat?" asked Norman, moving to the head of the table.

Simon sat down, further away from Norman than he would have liked, but the other chairs seemed to have been already taken by Simon's 'team' and the inner core of the Board. Simon began to feel uneasy and unsure. For the first time in his working life he felt at a loss to understand where he was heading. He didn't like to be taken off guard. He was a quiet planner, in control, acting subtly and often under the radar. His quiet determination had helped him to this point, but now he couldn't work out what was happening. He had had no warning, no premonition. He wondered to himself if he had been too absorbed with the Hong Kong plan, been out of the country for too long and away from HQ. Had he missed something? Had Norman not kept him in the loop, and if not why not?

He started to feel hot and felt the material of his suit sticking to his legs. He knew that if he took off his jacket he would have sweat marks under his arms. He stupidly started to question why he had ever bought the blue shirt, which he knew would show dark blue patches of sweat in the heat. He looked around the table. The core members looked as though they knew what was happening; they didn't look concerned. In fact, they looked resigned but contented. His team was looking relaxed and actually smiling. What did they know, he thought. What could possibly be making them feel secure when inside he was feeling anxious?

The coffee he had had on the train was starting to work through him and he wished he had taken a toilet break before coming up to the boardroom. He felt uncomfortable.

Norman took off his watch and he placed it in front of him on the table - a sign that the meeting was to start.

"Thank you, gentlemen, for this early start, and my apologies for not giving you more of a warning," he began, looking around the room. "As you are all aware, our project in Hong Kong is going well. Simon and his team have worked hard in the development and planning of the new factory and the signs are that we will be up and running within the month, as planned. Once the factory is working to full capacity our productivity worldwide is expected to increase significantly, and that will mean that our overall profitability will increase. The opportunity to make the same clothes more cheaply will inevitably mean that we will have the money to expand still further globally. As you are aware, our on-line business is also in the pipeline, and the team leading that aspect have ensured that our profitability will increase still further. Our factory in Hong Kong will be able to provide the goods cheaply and enable us to meet our orders both in the shops and on-line," continued Norman, becoming quite excited and enthusiastic.

Simon looked over to Greg, whom he had known for over fifteen years. A wizard with the computers, keen and full of enthusiasm. Like him, he had built himself up through the ranks. Simon acknowledged that he had come in as a graduate with a degree in IT, but he had started at the bottom and gradually got to know the company and its systems. It was no surprise to anyone that he had been given the task of setting up the on-line business, and with his success had come a place on the Board.

"Such is our success," continued Norman, "that it is inevitable, I suppose, that we would attract interest from our competitors. They like what they see and want to be a part of the action, our action. Of course, we are a relatively small fish in a large pond but over the years we have quietly got on with our jobs, forever expanding and subtly moving forwards. The sort of characteristics which are epitomised in many of the people around this table."

Yes, thought Simon that is it: quietly and subtly moving forwards. That is what he had been doing all his life, and that characteristic had been welcomed by the Board.

"We now move forward," continued Norman, "into the next stage. As you are aware, we have, over the last few years, slowly and subtly been bringing new people in to help us adapt and change to embrace the new world. To assist us with global thoughts and development. To take advantage of the Internet age and the demands of the next generation. We cannot stand still. We believe that our strategic planning has continued to enable us to thrive in a difficult market. We have taken important decisions and bold decisions to move forward and seek alternatives. Change and the will to embrace it. We have done this by evolving, using the old and trusted and bringing in the new and enthusiastic, teaching us about different methods and ways and how to manage them. Members of the Board, I am proud to have been a part of this evolution. I am also proud to inform you that we have received a take-over bid from one of our greatest competitors, World Wide Wardrobe (WWW). You will all have heard of them. A very successful and highly profitable business. Our inner core Board members and major shareholders have voted to accept their offer.

There will, of course, be changes. Many of us will be finishing and many of us will be given an opportunity to further develop our skills and career under a new and exciting management. As you can tell from their name, their emphasis is on global and

Internet selling. They have made significant strides in furthering this important aspect of our trade and have been looking for some time to take over a profitable and developing manufacturing company.

Our Hong Kong arm encouraged them to pitch for us with an offer, which, quite frankly, we would have been fools to reject. Each of you will individually have the opportunity to discuss with me how this move is to affect your future. I am setting up meetings throughout the day and my PA will hand to you, as you leave, an envelope setting out your individual circumstances and the time when I can meet with you. I would like to thank you all sincerely for the work and effort you have put into developing this company. We must now look forward, not backward, and see how we can embrace the future."

With that, the Chairman sat down. All the Board members looked around at each other, no-one knowing what the other was thinking. For Simon it was clear that some round the table were already aware of their individual fate. Some looked nervous and worried. Others sat there with grins on their faces, looking smug and contented.

The Chairman's PA opened the door. "Morning, gentlemen. This way please," she said loudly and confidently.

Everyone got up and moved towards her. They were each handed an envelope. "A bit like receiving your 'A' Level results," joked one of them nervously.

Simon didn't know about that. He had never taken 'A' Levels and so for him this was the first time that he had been in such a position. He normally felt organised, as if his whole life was part of a plan. But this moment was not in his plan. Why, he thought to himself, hadn't the Chairman given him a heads-up? He had thought they were friends. He had known him throughout his time at the company and thought that the Chairman valued his experience and commitment. Who else, Simon thought, knew as much as he did about the company? From the basement to the top floor he had slowly worked through each department. Who else could say that? But deep down Simon wondered if that was enough any longer. He had seen new people come straight into top positions, not needing to work up from the bottom. People with qualifications but no experience. His Hong Kong team, for example. They had only been with the company for at most two years. Simon had had a niggling doubt about them throughout this time of working with them. It wasn't envy of their sparkling degrees and MBAs. It wasn't their charm and ease of fitting in wherever they were. It was the way they seemed to assume that that was enough. That they didn't need the experience. That their enthusiasm and qualifications in business management would carry them through. Simon had weighed this up in his head and decided that it would not be enough. He had always been confident in his relationship with the Chairman and his loyalty throughout his working life to the company. Was this, he thought, going to be enough?

Each one of them made his way to the lifts and they divided themselves automatically into three groups to make their respective ways back to their own offices: Marketing, Finance, and Management. No-one opened his envelope. The envelopes remained stuck in their hands. Simon felt his envelope going limp between his fingers. He knew he was sweating under his expensive suit. His smart blue shirt would have big dark patches under his arms. For the first time in his life he wanted to be anywhere but in this building, a building he had loved from the age of sixteen, a building he felt he knew well, every pane of glass and every carpet tile and every pot plant.

"Rum carry-on, this," said one of his colleagues in the lift. "Did you suspect anything?" he continued to the others in the lift.

"No, not a thing," they replied.

"Come on, Simon," said one of them, "you must have known something. You are the Chairman's right-hand man, aren't you?"

"Not this time," Simon replied. He didn't want to talk to anyone. Fortunately, it was only two floors down for him to his office and he was able to escape quickly. He put the envelope in his pocket as he left the lift and walked over to his room.

Everything OK?" shouted the same girl who had told him about the meeting.

"Fine, yes," Simon said, trying to sound normal and confident. He walked into his room and closed the door.

He sat down behind his desk and took out the envelope. He put it in front of him and looked at it. It was crumpled in the corner where his sweaty fingers had held it. His head started to hurt and he wondered if he was going to get a migraine. He knew he had his tablets in the drawer and he checked. Yes, they were there. He then carefully opened the envelope, delicately unsticking it with his fingers. He took out the letter and slowly started to read the words on the paper. "As a result of the takeover of this company by World Wide Wardrobe, there will inevitably be some changes. We have tried to limit the number of redundancies but inevitably these will occur. Unfortunately, you will be part of this redundancy process. Very favourable packages will be on offer and the Chairman would like to discuss this with you today at ..."

Simon stopped reading the letter. He did not want to know and was unable to take it in. He felt confused and let down and cast out. For the first time he felt at a loss. He picked up his briefcase and walked to the lift, not looking behind him.

Eleanor

Eleanor walked with purpose through the barriers, hoping that her high heels would manage the fifteen-minute walk to the bank. She knew that it would be easier in trainers but could not quite come to terms with the business suit-and-trainers look. Some women managed it but they did look ridiculous, she thought. She wondered how long it would be before she had to resort to flat shoes, the precursor to the trainer. She looked at some of the other women getting off the train. She recognised many of them but had never spoken to them. She recognised their clothes and their shoes. She noticed when they had a new suit or had had a haircut.

She had been doing this journey for so long that she felt part of the train itself. She knew every broken seat, every toilet door which wouldn't lock, every stain on the carpet and every guard, the surly ones and the pleasant ones, the friendly ones and the power-crazy ones. She always felt that she used the time well. She settled down as soon as she got on, and took out her make up bag. Taking care no-one saw her (the train never being very full when she got on), she carefully applied her make-up in the same way she had been doing for thirty years. She sometimes felt she should invest in a new product but having once tried a make-up counter makeover she felt it was a waste of money. She could get as good a look herself using the products she had always used. She then always took out some work so that she could start the day well and on top of the game. The job was hard and seemed to get harder: always more reports to write, advice to give, calculations to make. Making Business Manager of a leading bank branch in the City was, she felt, the highest she could go. She was proud of herself and valued every moment, working up from the graduate training intake, taking the MBA, and keeping going throughout had been tough but worth it.

She left the station and walked into the outside world. She was always aware of the weather - cold, warm, wet, dry - and tried to make sure she would be dressed appropriately. She often wished she could find an alternative to the briefcase, as it was often very heavy, but she couldn't quite bring herself to using a backpack. It would ruin the shoulder pads on her jackets. They also looked scruffy and inappropriate to her. The weather was fine, so she set off feeling relatively comfortable.

She had a difficult day ahead. She had several customer meetings and an Area Manager meeting at the end of the day. She hoped she would be able to make the six o'clock train home as normal, but she knew that it was often touch and go. She preferred to walk to the bank. The fresh air felt better than the stale, humid air of the Tube. The bodies squashed together in a small space trying desperately to ignore each other. The ones with music playing through headphones really annoyed her. Why, she thought, don't they realise that everyone else can hear the music as well as a continuous base thud? She also felt that by the time she had walked down to the platform and waited for the train she could have been halfway down the street to the bank. She therefore walked. She arrived at the bank in good time as the doors were being unlocked. She walked through and headed towards her office.

"Morning, Eleanor," called a couple of the girls from behind the counters.

"Morning," she replied, looking straight ahead.

"Why doesn't she ever stop and chat?" one girl said to the other.

"Focused," was the reply from the girl, who was admiring the nail art on her fingernails. "She's got a job to do and the only way is up for her," she continued. "Have you noticed that she only ever wants to talk to the men from Head Office? She isn't interested in us. We aren't useful to her. But she's the same with everyone here. No real friends."

At that moment the first customer came through the door and the day started.

Eleanor met a few others on the way to her room. She briefly talked about the weather and then settled into her chair and turned her computer on. She checked her calendar and the times of her customer meetings and pulled out the files to remind herself of their details. Her report for the meeting later on was prepared and she could tweak that at lunchtime while eating her home-made sandwiches.

She enjoyed seeing customers. She enjoyed talking with them about their businesses and their lives and how they had arrived at this point. She half-felt she lived vicariously through them. They all excited her. One or two she didn't particularly like, but overall the customers she met were interesting people. She admired their attitude to life. They were on the whole optimistic and enthusiastic. You had to be if you were in business. Of course, some businesses failed. She sympathised with these people but had to move on. She wanted committed businessmen who wanted to move forward with healthy accounts, strong business plans and a willingness to take risks. One of her best tasks was to read through their annual accounts, look at their figures and do comparisons. She encouraged these people to keep their business plans up to date, forever looking to the future. But she also wanted successful businesses: those who had plans to expand, develop and diversify. With the help of the bank they could do this and it was her job to identify those businesses which were going to do just that. The bank could do well out of them and she personally would benefit. The bank did not want those which failed, collapsing with debt, owing vast sums of money to others, including the bank. She had had one or two customers go belly-up. She had tried to advise them early on but it was a fine line between moving forward and taking risks. Taking too many risks and failing.

She looked at the graph she kept on the wall and did a comparison of her customers, those who succeeded and those who failed. She tried to find a common thread, a similarity in type of business or type of person. She had for the last eighteen months at least been constrained by Head Office directives. No more lending. Keep things tight. Look after the customers as they are. No risks until we are out of the recession. But it was a double or triple-dip recession. She knew that some of her customers were struggling. All three of her customer meetings today were with business owners who had been with the bank for years. She knew what they would be wanting and she knew what Head Office directives allowed her to do. She checked her computer for new business for the last month. She realised that the figures were significantly down. Not as many people were starting up businesses. Not surprising really, as there was no money around to get them started. Bad news for them but also bad news for her. She knew that the Area Manager at the meeting this afternoon would expect to go through the figures, schedules and graphs, and would be looking for explanations.

Her telephone rang and she picked it up quickly.

"Hello, Eleanor. Your first appointment is here. Mr Nigel Jones of Jones and Sons, Tailors. Shall I bring him through to you?" the receptionist enquired.

"Yes, please," said Eleanor, ready for the first customer. She checked her make-up in her handbag mirror and went out of her office to greet him. His file was already on her desk and all the reports in order.

"Good morning, Mr Jones," she said. "How are you today?"

"Could be better," he replied. "Difficult times, Miss Collins. I hope you're going to be able to help us out," he said, quietly and hopefully.

"Shall we look at the figures, then?" replied Eleanor. "I have all the day-to-day accounts and projections from last month. Do you have the up-to-date ones with you, Mr Jones?" she enquired.

"Yes," he replied, "I've brought everything I could lay my hands on: the order book, invoices and receipts. Unfortunately I lost my big contract which I expected to be working on next month. A wedding. I was supposed to be doing all the suits, wedding and bridesmaids' dresses and mother of the bride - a big order. I had sourced the fabrics, spent ages with the customers discussing designs. I thought I had costed it out well. It worked out to be half of what they might have to pay elsewhere and a fraction of what the well-known designers would have charged. Then, blow me, a phone call last week cancelling."

"Did they give any reason?" asked Eleanor, wondering why such an order should be lost.

"They said they could no longer afford it all," he said. "I think the couple are still getting married. But they said that they themselves were struggling financially. The chap is a businessman and I think he is finding it tough out there. I think they were going to put the money into the deposit for a flat rather than buy clothes they would wear only once. I can understand them really but it doesn't help me. In fact, the story could be told over and over again. I had an order for several ball-gowns for a big charity ball. Do you know, they cancelled the ball. They actually cancelled it because not enough people had bought tickets. Too expensive, you see. A luxury. Even though all the proceeds were to go to charity, people don't have the money at the moment. They can't afford to spend unnecessarily even though it is for a good cause. It has a knock-on effect, though. If it carries on like this I shall have to lay off one or two of my staff." He looked at Eleanor with sad eyes, eyes which had seen a lot of problems in the past but nothing like the present ones.

"What about your routine orders?" asked Eleanor. "The contract with the chain store how's that going?" She looked at him hopefully, trying to raise his spirits.

"Well," he said, "I still have it but it doesn't pay. To keep the contract I have had to quote so low that there is very little profit in it. Overseas competition, you see. Cheap clothes made on the cheap in India or China. No-one seems to want bespoke any more. They're happy to buy cheap and cheerful from a chain store, and the owners of these chain stores can knock you down in price because they have the power. If I didn't do the work they could find someone who could, or they would outsource abroad. This is the way it's going, Miss Collins. Unless you're in with the wealthy crowd, and design and make for the celebrities who can pay, it's difficult to make a living."

Mr Jones looked sad and depressed. He had been a tailor all his life, trained by his father who had worked at a time when many people wanted bespoke clothing. His father had died leaving a thriving business to his son. Now this Mr Jones was struggling and Eleanor suspected that the third generation Mr Jones would have to contemplate a different career.

"Well, Mr Jones," said Eleanor, "we're going to have to formulate a plan. What I want from you is an up-to-date business plan. Your figures aren't good, are they? You can't carry on in this way. You're nearly at the top of your overdraft, and as you're well aware, at the moment, in this economic climate, the bank is reluctant to extend overdraft facilities or grant loans. What you have to do is focus and diversify. Look for new markets, new ways of making money. Be creative. Are you in any marketing or networking groups? Are you advertising? You need an expert marketer, perhaps, who could advise you."

"Miss Collins," replied Mr Jones, "I'm a tailor, not a businessman. I make clothes. I love making clothes. I love the feel of the fabric. I like cutting out. I like to structure a garment and see it grow. It is what I do." Mr Jones did not know what else to say. He desperately needed the bank to keep him going, to extend his overdraft and give him a small loan to tide him over.

"Mr Jones," said Eleanor, a little frustrated, "come back in a week's time with a specific business plan. Bring with you a schedule of all your personal assets, together with all your daily accounts sheets and your order book. I will use these in my discussions with Head Office and see if together we can formulate a six-point plan. I cannot hold out much hope but will give you this last chance. One week's time. I hope to see an improvement."

Mr Jones got up. Eleanor ushered him towards the door. The meeting was over. He did not feel reassured. He wondered why the future of his father's firm was resting in the lap of a woman in a small, sterile room in a small branch office of a bank. He seemed resigned. He shook her hand and disappeared. Both of them knew it was hopeless. He had no more security to offer. He had borrowed against his house to its full value. He had no savings and no investments. He only had his workshop, which he rented, and his sewing machines. If those went he couldn't continue. He walked out of the bank slowly and quietly.

Eleanor knew she had two more customers in similar situations this morning. She tried to work out a structure as to how to deal with them. The more she looked at their files, the worse it became. First a tailor, then a wine merchant, fighting against the ever-increasing power of the supermarkets, and lastly the jewellery repair business from a few doors up the road. She checked through their accounts. There was a common feature. None of them had moved with the times. All were facing a changing society and marketplace. She couldn't understand why they had closed their eyes to what had been happening. She had told them enough times at their regular meetings. She had tried to work with them and set up plans and targets, but none had succeeded in reaching a satisfactory solution.

By two o'clock she had seen them all, and was feeling quite despondent. She made herself a coffee and got out her sandwiches. It was a watershed. She never stopped working, of course: she didn't have time, so she continued to eat and write up her reports on the morning's customers. She led a solitary life. Whilst she enjoyed the job and the customers, she felt isolated at the bank. The cashiers obviously did not want to have much to do with her. She was in a

potential and that you were the one, with respect, the age and experience to do just that. Though a small branch, it is nonetheless central and relatively busy. You were part of a three-year plan and that three-year period has come to an end. If the branch is not making money then it is no longer viable. You have enough experience to understand that money cannot be made from bankrupt customers. The figures speak for themselves. The majority of your small business customers are going to fail and close down. We don't make money from those sorts. We lose money. We make money from overdrafts and loans and the customers' being able to service those liabilities. Of course, Miss Collins, I don't have to tell *you* this."

Eleanor tried to interrupt him, and started to pull out graphs and the comparisons which she had done over the last few evenings. She believed that many of her customers could turn their businesses around.

"The problem, Miss Collins," Mr Bates continued, "is that you have become too close to these people.

You have allowed yourself to look at the individuals and not the figures. We are not in this for sympathy and understanding. We are in it to make money, Miss Collins, and that is what you have singularly failed to do. Decisions should have been made weeks ago to pull the plug on a number of these customers. We have continued to leave ourselves wide open to loss. We believe at Head Office that sadly the branch has failed as regards business development. Your reports and graphs are fine and I do appreciate the effort you have put in. Sadly, it is not enough."

Eleanor looked at him and couldn't work out where the conversation was heading. She started to feel uncomfortable. Her hands were becoming sticky and she felt perspiration forming on her upper lip. She knew he was right. She had let herself get too involved. She didn't understand why. She liked figures, not people. Why, she thought, had this happened?

"In the circumstances," Mr Bates continued, "Miss Collins, we have decided that there will be no business development manager at this branch. You will be transferred back to Head Office to work in the Debt Recovery team. The department is headed up by a very good new recruit, who, I am sure, will find your graphs and skill with figures most helpful. Back to figures, Miss Collins, and away from people, that is what you need. That is where your skills lie. However, as I'm sure you are aware, if you do not relish this prospect, then the bank has for several months now been looking for voluntary redundancies. There are good packages on offer and you may feel that it's time to move on, take on new challenges or spend more time with your family. Do let me know your decision by tomorrow at nine o'clock. Good afternoon, Miss Collins."

And he was gone. Out of the door into the rain. He didn't even shake her hand. He didn't know anything about her and clearly had not looked at her personal file in HR. She didn't have a family. Her parents had passed away several years ago. She had spent five years caring for her father until his death, and didn't seem to have had time for herself ever. No time to find a husband. Work and figures and graphs had always seemed enough.

She sat behind her desk feeling at a loss. She did not know what to do or how to react. She logged off her computer and put away all the files, graphs, statements and the reports she had prepared. She took her bag from her desk drawer and walked out of the bank and into the rain.

Gerry

Gerry loved his bicycle. He liked the way it folded up small and he could stow it away in the baggage section. Once out of the train it quickly came back to life with a flick and a turn. Power, he thought. Total control. He always tried to be careful as he carried it in its constricted state off the train. The mishap with the smart lady when he had caught her legs, leaving an oily patch, had taught him to be extra-careful. But, once the bike had blossomed into its own on the platform he felt liberated. He walked slowly with his bike up the platform and manoeuvred through the barrier. This was always difficult with his helmet and backpack, but he was careful and gently managed to get through, picking his season ticket out of the exit barrier with his teeth. It always remained there while he put his helmet on. Carefully putting his ticket away into its special holder and into his zip-up pocket on his waterproof cycle jacket, he was then ready for the day.

He looked forward to the freedom of the road. Along with many other cyclists, he negotiated the heavy traffic outside the station. Gradually moving to the front of the traffic at the traffic lights, he eagerly waited to head off as if in a pack at the front of the queue. He always stayed on the outside of the road, not the kerbside. He had learnt the hard way of the dangers of kerb-hugging. A bus had very nearly clipped him and knocked him over. There were too many cycling casualties and too many deaths. He daily passed a "ghost bike" attached to a railing outside the station. Someone always put fresh flowers on it. He had recently seen another one at a crossing just a little further up the road. Reminders of dear ones lost to the wheels of a bus or car.

Gerry was a careful and methodical man in all aspects of his life. He was renowned for it. A safe pair of hands, people would say. Reliable, dependable and solid. Gerry didn't know if he liked this. He always felt there was someone else inside him struggling to get out, but frightened actually to escape. He quietly remained in character with the burning sensation safely stored inside.

But on the road he was free. He felt daily that he was escaping. He went as fast as anyone could in the centre of the capital. Whether it was windy, raining or sunny, he enjoyed the weather in his face and on his legs. He felt liberated from everything and everybody, as if he had the power to cycle on and on and out of his humdrum life and into infinity. 'To infinity and beyond!' He had enjoyed watching films with his children. They were both grown up now but he had kept Buzz Lightyear in the bottom drawer of a wardrobe as a reminder of happier days. The children had long ago left home, living their own lives. He envied the fact that they had gone out into the world, pursuing dreams in faraway places.

Then his wife had gone to pursue her own dreams. Gerry felt he had stayed put and just financed it all. Day after day following the same routine, the same routes. The only difference was the new bike. He had treated himself a few years ago to a state-of-the-art collapsible speedbike. He had felt sad putting out his old one for the scrap-man, but had told himself that it had had a good life: twenty years of intercity travel in the guard's van. Times change and Gerry had felt able to justify a new bike. It could travel with him in the compartment, folding up into the size of a suitcase. The ease with which it morphed into a proper-sized bike daily brought a smile to his face. The highlights of his day were to ride to and from work. There seemed to be camaraderie between the cyclists: one big pack at the front of the traffic, ready to go as the lights changed. He never jumped the lights like some people. No point, he thought. It was asking for trouble. But he did set off as soon as he could.

Bikes came in all shapes and sizes and colours. He noticed the women on the old-fashioned bicycles with baskets attached to the handlebars. He thought in a nostalgic way that he liked the idea of a smart lady on a bike like this. Very often they were dressed smartly. Sometimes they even wore high heels and had handbags in the basket. They didn't wear helmets and they looked like a vision of perfection and serenity. Some had flowing scarves and skirts and he often worried about them getting caught in the wheels. But one common feature of all of them was the determination to move forward with the traffic, their faces set against the weather and fighting the road challenges. It was one big club. Hunting in a pack.

Eventually Gerry arrived at his office. He worked at the National Railway Head Office in Administration. He had been there since leaving school. He liked the familiarity of it all: the routine and the systems. He was now in charge of timetables. He was proud of his work. He could tell you the times of trains anywhere in the country. He relished the prospect of the biannual release of the new timetables. Working out tables and graphs, timings and connections. It was a solitary occupation, as over the years his department had been reduced in numbers. Fewer trains and faster trains meant that the timetables didn't change so much. But he had been working on the Eurostar connections and the highlight of the last few years had been a trip to Paris to liaise with his French counterpart. He had really felt part of the future and for one of the few times in his life he had felt that he was doing something important. It had been downhill since then, back to the mundane. But the office knew that someone had to do it and that Gerry was the man.

He arrived and quickly collapsed up his bike. It fitted well into the lift. Unfortunately, however, the lift had a very large mirror and each morning he looked into it and saw the reflection of a bright red, sweaty face, with beads of sweat running down the sides of his forehead. As he took off his helmet each day he witnessed hair stuck to his head with sweat. What a sight! he thought to himself each day, and smiled. He always hoped that there wouldn't be anyone else in the lift with him to witness this daily horror. He also knew that his back was sweaty because of his backpack.

Twelfth floor and straight into the men's loos. He then proceeded to strip off and swill down. He felt he morphed, just like his bike, which he usually left in the corridor outside the loos. He emerged with a clean shirt and suit, a little crumpled as they had been in the backpack, and hair brushed back, wet with the water swilled over it. He often thought it would be good if there were a shower in the office, but then again he didn't know if he would have the time before compulsory clocking-in for such a luxury. He picked up his bike, then he and the bike and walked over to his workspace.

"Morning, Gerry. Good trip in?" One of his colleagues shouted out the same comment each morning, and always looked smart and neat as if he himself had been ironed. Gerry hardly acknowledged him, as he always felt too embarrassed by his own look. Relief came when he got to his workspace. Next to him sat Ralph, a runner, who arrived each morning at his desk in his running kit. "Hi, Ralph, how are things?" Gerry called out. "Was the run in good today?

"Brilliant, Gerry," he replied. "Perfect day - cool and crisp, lots of runners out today. My time's getting better and the build-up to the marathon is going really well. I must change, though, otherwise the boss will scream at me yet again."

Ralph kept a suit hanging up behind a cupboard door, always the same suit and often a shirt and tie underneath it. Ralph didn't seem to bother about a shower or a swill-down. He daily got changed there in front of Gerry, whilst downing a glass of water and eating a bowl of cornflakes. Gerry laughed. He regularly wondered if their joint body odour was the reason why very few people came over to their area of the office.

"Hey, Gerry, have you heard there is a departmental meeting today at four o'clock? Something about restructuring and development.

Look at your e-mails. Apparently all, the floor has to attend. I hope it's nothing serious," called Ralph through a mouthful of his cereal.

"Oh, it won't be," replied Gerry. "They're always having them. Someone new comes in at the top and thinks he has to make his mark. It usually settles down. I don't know why they can't just leave us all alone. We get the job done."

"I know, Gerry," Ralph replied, "but the government does seem to be very interested in costings and cutbacks. The railway isn't the most popular at the moment, is it?" he asked, smiling.

"Let them look at the Health Service," replied Gerry. "There's more work to be done there. Why is it that the government always wants to interfere and make headlines at the expense of someone?"

He turned on his computer and logged on. It had become a habit. Changing his password every quarter. Going through his e-mails. Never anything exciting, just boring work. But it made him feel secure. He liked routine and familiarity. He hated it when people left, but then hardly anyone did. Most stayed as long as possible and retired, with their card and send-off present and brief speech from the Head of Department and, of course, the pension and cheap rail travel for life. Not a bad deal, he thought. He had always liked tables and graphs. He enjoyed timetables, the neatness and structure of them. He liked to think that at a certain time at a certain place a certain train would be coming into the station, picking people up and leaving according to the timetable. He especially liked it twice a year when he and his team delivered the new timetable. Obviously, changes were usually minor but he liked the way the new times looked on the timetable. The subtle realignment. He liked the image that the figures created, the patterns on the page and the fact that everyone who wanted to know about the trains looked at *his* figures and *his* patterns.

Gerry's computer had fired up and there were his e-mails. He scrolled down to find the one Ralph had mentioned. There it was: the Head of Department writing to everyone in the department calling them to a meeting.

"I hope we get tea and biscuits," he said to Ralph.

"Bound to," replied Ralph. "At four o'clock everyone is ready for a cuppa. Hope they give us chocolate biscuits, not boring digestives, stale leftovers from this morning's meetings with the planners," he added.

"What meeting with the planners?" asked Gerry. "I thought we had had all our meetings to discuss next year's rail plans and how we are all to be affected."

"Don't you read all your e-mails, Gerry?" Ralph laughed. "Your head is permanently in the figures. You should keep abreast of the gossip. Kate on Reception told me that there have been a series of meetings over the last couple of weeks with even the Minister of Transport arriving."

"I bet *he* got chocolate biscuits," chuckled Gerry.

"Bound to have," laughed Ralph, "and probably ate the lot. By the look of him he likes a packet or two of custard creams or chocolate digestives." Ralph pondered. "But I do wonder," he said, "why there have been so many high-level meetings. Kate says that they have been going in and out with lots of folders and men in grey suits all looking terribly official."

"You talk too much with Kate," said Gerry. "She doesn't know anything."

"Maybe not," replied Ralph "but it's always good to spend half an hour with her finding out what she doesn't know!" Ralph laughed again.

Gerry had this picture of Ralph standing at the reception desk, sweat pouring down his face, his running Lycra steaming, and Ralph in running gear and trainers trying to chat up the receptionist. Gerry smiled. "Don't you ever give up, Ralph? Why do you have to chat up everything in a skirt with long, straight-ironed, blonde hair?" he asked.

"It's fun," replied Ralph, "and in any event one of these days I may score. Always the optimist, Gerry, and it beats Internet dating. You never know what you are going to get on that. In my experience, the reality differs fundamentally from the picture and description on the screen and in fact…"

Ralph went on and on and Gerry switched off. It was like this every morning. Ralph was good fun but impossible to shut up. Gerry got out his notes and started to work. He was looking into the timetables for the inter-city mainline. He knew that a number of stops had had to be cancelled to make the journey time quicker and supposedly more efficient. He wondered what all those travellers would think when they realised that the trains had been drastically cut from the smaller stations and the larger stations were getting the quicker trains. They would not be pleased. Fortunately, it wasn't his job to consider people's feelings. He was no good with emotion, only figures. He hid himself in figures. He blocked out all need to think about human reactions to anything. Whenever he did think about people and emotions, he became sad and he didn't like to be sad. You couldn't trust emotion, he thought. Always got you into tricky situations. Much better to stick to figures.

By lunchtime Gerry had managed to sort out at least half of the new timetable; working with the stations and crews he had calculated to the minute the times of pulling in and pulling out, the times to pick up passengers and the savings to be made in time and cost. He had been working on this project for months - in fact, since the last timetable change. It was a tricky line because it was very busy all the time. Not just commuters but travellers to the city, business, pleasure, holidays, weekends away. He had until the end of the month to bring it all together and so far he was pleased with his graphs and plans. He walked out of the office into the rain and wind. He liked going for a walk at lunchtime. He tried to choose a different park bench to eat his sandwiches. He left the office, clutching his plastic sandwich box and thermos flask. He was always glad that he had made them at home and brought them in. He didn't have to waste time queuing for a plastic sandwich and coffee at some extortionate price in a trendy bar or cafe or takeaway. He planned his lunchtime during his mid-morning coffee break with Ralph. Ralph preferred the office canteen. He liked to eye up all the girls, checking out any new talent, as he would say. Gerry didn't know why he bothered. His own view of girls and marriage was tarnished. His own wife had left years ago. She said she was bored, but it didn't stop her taking half of his house, half of his pension and half of his salary. But he still had his bike and his job and so he was satisfied.

After a couple of hours after lunch working on his graphs, he joined Ralph and the rest of the team for the meeting. He felt ready for a cup of tea and was quite looking forward to the free biscuits. There was a massive surge to the table at the back of the room where the biscuits had been laid out in front of the huge tea and coffee dispensers. Only shortbreads and Garibaldis left for Ralph and Gerry.

"Bloody typical," cried Ralph. "I'd got quite ready for a chocolate digestive. Hopes dashed as ever, eh, Gerry?"

Gerry smiled and sat down in the back row. Chairs had been laid out in semi-circular rows, and the Head of Department and Chief Executive were at the front. The Chief used his spoon to bring order. It was like a party atmosphere. Gerry thought they were all going to get bonuses or at the very least be let in on all the secret meetings which had been taking place.

"Ladies and gentlemen," he opened in a loud voice, seemingly full of biscuit, "I would like to thank you all for attending today. Some of you may have noticed the various meetings myself and my team have been having, and we feel it is important to fill you all in on the recent developments. As you know, the government has taken on board all the requirements of providing an up-to-date, effective and efficient rail service. We have a long way to go. There are bids to build new lines and routes, to commission new trains to compete with the European ones, and do all this within a limited departmental and business budget. You will be aware that the government has had to take over control of some routes as the privatisation has not worked and was proving problematical. Our company has grown out of the old British Rail. We are a service to the railways. We also have to deliver a cost-effective service. This means that for some there are wonderful opportunities. For others it will mean considering alternative career paths and also, for some, retirement, and early retirement will be the only options. We are here with the HR Department to work with you to achieve the best solution for you all as individuals. We all must move forward and embrace change. The recession is affecting everyone and we all have to adapt."

Gerry started to fidget. He brushed off the crumbs of his biscuit, which had fallen down his jumper.

Retirement, he thought. He felt hot inside and started to sweat. He was sixty-four years old and had always thought that he would not have to think about retirement until at least sixty-five and with the new ageism law he had rather hoped, if he kept quiet, that he could carry on forever. His ideal would have been to pass away at his desk over his timetables. He didn't have anything else. They were his life.

Everyone was invited to move towards the HR table to fix up a meeting with one of the team. He had never had anything to do with HR before, apart from one week when he had had 'flu and they told him to fill in a self-certificate form, he had had no need. Even through his divorce he had had no need to call upon their 'compassionate services'. Forty-six years he had been employed by them and caused no trouble.

Gerry fixed up his appointment for ten minutes after Ralph the following day. "I'm off,"said Ralph, "if they give me a good deal. What about you, Gerry?"

"No doubt they want to pension me off," replied Gerry glumly.

They left the room, Ralph grabbing a handful of the remaining biscuits and stuffing them in his pocket.

A subdued bunch arrived back on their floor. No one really knew what to do.

"They can't do without us," several people said. "How would they work out the timetables?"

"Computers!" shouted Ralph. "They can do bloody everything these days."

Gerry decided to pick up his kit and go home. He had had enough and didn't want to look at the computer again. He had never had to think about alternatives. His job had been his security. He felt he was being cast out to sea. An unknown sea and he couldn't touch the bottom.

The Journey Home

The roads and pavements were packed. The buses could hardly move along and taxis idled, looking at the charges ticking over while the customer sat anxiously in the back. Cyclists, brightly coloured in their outfits and helmets, meandered in and out of the stationary traffic. Children ran along the pavements; others were on skateboards and scooters, bags thrown casually on their backs, harassed parents keeping pace. Pedestrians moved forward at everyone's pace, unable to rush unless they noticed a gap in the crowd. Runners and dawdlers, tourists and commuters, students and children, travellers with wheelie suitcases, making it doubly difficult to move along, shoppers with gleaming carrier bags of designer outfits, workers with plastic carrier bags full of the supermarket's ready meals and night-time provisions.

In amongst this crowd were four very individual people heading for the same station to catch their regular 17.52 train home, usually with an eye on their watch for split-second timing, knowing the time when they had to be at a certain place, platform of the underground, crossroads or traffic lights. Years and years of the same route, passing the same places and the same people. But tonight it was different. All four didn't have that feeling of rushing and busyness. They made their respective ways in a foggy cloud, their minds on other things. Yes, all the places and people were still there at the same time, but they did not feel a part of it any more. The routine which had formed their lives was being taken away from them. This morning, everything was normal. Tonight, everything was different.

They arrived at the station and picked up the free newspaper from the same man in the same place.

"Hello," he said. "Good day?" he asked as he handed over the paper.

"Yes, thank you," was the automatic reply.

What else was there to say? Where could they begin, and would the newspaper man really be interested? Yes, he saw them every day but he didn't know them and probably didn't want to. They were each one part of a huge, anonymous crowd. He saw thousands of people every day and no doubt said the same thing to all of them. Habit and conversation but no real interest. What would he have said if the reply had been "Well, no, actually. I've just lost my job"? The newspaper man would have been embarrassed and would not have wanted such intimacy.

The train was in the station and boarding on Platform One. Three minutes to go to departure. Crowds of passengers were scurrying to the train, fearful of missing it. They were the tourists. The commuters knew that they had an exact number of minutes to go before it left the station, and were able to time exactly when they had to be going through the barriers and when they had to be stepping onto the train. On the first coach, First Class, and walk through to Standard Class. With any luck there would be some leftover newspapers from the morning to pick up on the way through. It was nice, normally, walking through First Class. Bigger seats, free drinks and an 'at-seat service'. Not worth the extra cost of the ticket, they all thought. First Class was full of people who didn't pay for their own tickets: corporate men, railway and government officials; ladies who lunch on a shopping spree, Dads with contact visits to their children who needed the extra space and help from the staff.

Gerry was on first. He had left the office early, taking his bike into the men's toilets and changing into his cycling gear. When on the road he hadn't enjoyed the traffic, the buses or vans. He lingered at the traffic lights rather than cycling through with an eye on all the traffic. It seemed unreal, but then, he thought, why shouldn't I finish? Everything must end. He was nearly sixty-five, for God's sake. A new start, something different. But these thoughts couldn't beat the thoughts of despair and fright. He didn't know what else to do. He had never had time to think. He was always in motion with his timetables in his head. What useless information! The 20.15 from St Pancras or the 17.48 from Kings Cross will carry on without me, that's for sure, he thought. He cycled past the ghost bike and then stopped. He got off his bike and folded it up and walked the remaining fifty yards to the station.

"Early today, sir," said the newspaper man.

"Yes," he replied. "Skipped off work early."

"Well, see you tomorrow, sir," said the newspaper man.

Gerry didn't reply. He went through the ticket barriers and walked towards the platform. Too early for scurriers. He had a leisurely stroll to his carriage. Carefully climbing on with his bike, he had plenty of room to store the bike at the end luggage rack. He sat down. He plugged in his headphones as a matter of routine and closed his eyes.

Eleanor had left the bank so quickly and without thought that she had forgotten to take off her high heels and change into her walking shoes, which she usually did at the end of the day. Too late. She couldn't go back. She walked with purpose towards the station. She knew that by the time she reached the station her feet would be killing her after spending the whole day in high heels. Also she knew the heels would be even more worn-down. Her legs would be splashed with the rain puddles and her hair would be blown out of shape. Normally this would concern her and she would strive to ensure against all such eventualities. Tonight she wasn't bothered. For so long she had walked up and down these streets to and from work that she really felt she was on automatic pilot.

She didn't see the shops or the people. The one-man barber always busy with his one-chair, one-room business. The Indian corner shop with exotic fruits and veggies displayed outside. The Italian restaurant setting up the tables inside and out, chalking up today's specials. The broken paving-stones, the kids coming out of college, the runners with backpacks - all were unnoticed tonight. Normally they would all give Eleanor security and joy. Tonight they didn't exist.

She walked past the ghost bike and waited on the pavement at the crossing for the green man. Getting her season ticket out for the barriers seemed automatic to her. A life of routine and responsibility. A life of purpose revolving around her job.

But where had this taken her? Being dispensable, subject to someone else's whims. As if her lifetime of commitment to the bank had been for nothing. She walked towards the train and climbed into First Class. She looked around at the businessmen getting out their laptops, reading reports and talking with others about their deals, their plans, their meetings. They all looked successful in their snazzy suits and sharp shirts, shoes polished and hair slicked back. She had never made it to First Class. A brief period of travel to Head Office from the provincial bank during the 80's had been her highlight and only First Class experience. All expenses paid. Flavour of the month then. A rising star for the bank, nurtured and valued. What had happened, she thought. She wasn't too old, wasn't lacking in commitment. Where was her mistake? Perhaps that was it. Not approachable. She had taken it all too seriously, not giving herself time to have anything else in her life. She had been too focused and not seen the bigger picture. Of course she had never had a family to take her mind off her job. No husband or kids to do things with. It had never seemed necessary. She had never had the time. Even her annual holiday had been educational visits to cities around the world. She never turned off.

This was the real world. Demoted. Clearly not up to scratch. A failure in the bank's eyes. Shifted over to a boring run-of-the-mill job. She pushed her way through the train and sat down in her usual place and closed her eyes. No laptop out, no reading of reports, no plans. What was the point? She was yesterday's news.

Simon hadn't taken up the appointment at four o'clock to discuss his redundancy. He couldn't face it. Redundancy, he said to himself. How can I discuss that? I've been at this place all my life. I don't know anything else. He couldn't look at anyone and didn't want to see anyone. He hadn't seen the signs. He thought he was secure and that the men in charge had valued him for his loyalty, commitment and reliability. He resented the newcomers, those graduates with their easy smiles and confidence. Simon had always thought that it wouldn't matter. He knew the company inside out and had gained the confidence of everybody. The graduates had come in and taken over. The heads of the bosses had been turned by their smart ideas. Trendy ideas from their trendy business schools. PhDs and MBAs. What did that teach them? No, thought Simon, he knew what it was really like on the ground.

In the real world he knew what a company needed and how it ticked. No fancy ideas, just thoroughness. But deep down Simon felt inadequate. He had always felt inadequate. Personality and knowledge of the business can only take you so far. He had no qualifications. It hadn't mattered initially. But it did now. He walked to the door.

"Early night tonight, sir? Unlike you," commented the doorman.

"Yes," replied Simon. "Thought I'd give myself a treat."

"Just the thing, sir. Does you good now and then. Have a nice evening," said the doorman.

"Thank you," replied Simon. He liked the doorman. He was always so courteous. He had known him all his working life and he had always been the same. Polite and gentle. Never intrusive and always saying the right thing.

Simon walked into the fresh air. Everything as it always was. The taxis and the buses, a police siren in the distance, people pushing their way along the street. It was too early for the hordes of commuters coming out of the offices to make the pavements packed. It was too early for the train home. Simon turned right instead of left and walked down to the river. He had always liked this view. The whole of the capital clinging to the river and the river packed with boats, water-taxis and people. Along the side, tourists, joggers, dogs, schoolchildren on their visits, groups of Chinese people huddled around a tour guide, a group of Americans in trainers and ill-fitting trousers. Simon had never known what people did during the day. He had never experienced a day out of the office during normal working hours. Holidays were different. Taken abroad at a hotel and on a beach with the kids. It felt wrong. He felt naughty, as if he were stealing time and should be somewhere else. But there was nowhere else to go.

He sat down on a bench and stared at the view. He watched the water move downstream and didn't know what to do. He closed his eyes and thought about his wife and kids, the house and the swimming pool, his pride at achieving all of this. He thought of his father, long dead, and his advice. "Work hard and get good solid experience." He had done this, but in the end it hadn't been enough. He looked at his watch and realised that he must have been sitting there for over an hour. He would have to rush to get to the train. He walked automatically back up the street and past his office to the Tube. As he passed his office he felt sick. In fact, he thought he was going to *be* sick. He looked through the windows on the ground floor and saw some of the people having their meetings with HR. Everyone busy, everyone assessing what they were going to get and what they were going to do. Simon couldn't face it and resented being expected to face it.

He arrived at the Tube as a train was coming in. By now, the platform was packed and everyone was trying to squeeze on to the train. Simon knew he would somehow have to get on the train to get to the station in time for his train home. He just managed it as the Tube door was closing by giving one big push towards an obese lady who seemed to take up three-quarters of the space at the end of the carriage. A good job the doors closed, since he seemed to bounce off her and back on to the door. No-one spoke, each of them desperate to ensure they kept breathing in the confined space and kept away from the coughers and the sneezers.

The Tube arrived at the station and the doors opened. In one mass most of them fell onto the platform. It was unnecessary to walk, as they were all carried along together. Simon, as a matter of habit, got the Tube carriage which stopped exactly at the exit to the station, making it easier and quicker to get to the escalator and up to the mainline station. He moved along with the crowd and came up into the station concourse. He looked up at the board to find the platform and hurried to the train with a minute to spare. He jumped on to the first carriage, First Class. He had never made it to First Class but actually had never wanted to. He had been content to travel Business Class when he went to Hong Kong on business and put up with Standard Class at home when he was paying for himself. He walked through like he did every night and didn't see anyone. He found Standard and took his usual seat. He felt it was all unreal. Everything he was doing was the same as he had done every day all his life. This time, however, it was different.

By the time they left the Bank it was five o'clock and Anthony didn't go back to the office. He hailed the first cab he saw and climbed in the back. "The station, please," he instructed the driver.

"OK, mate, had a good day?" the driver enquired.

"Fine, thank you, as ever," Anthony responded.

The traffic was bad and Anthony noticed the charges increasing rapidly. He hadn't normally thought about the cost before, but, having had a grilling at the bank, for the first time he saw how ridiculously expensive cabs were. He thought about Gerry and his fold-up bike. No wonder he has one of those, he thought. It saves money. He had never thought about that aspect of Gerry before. He just thought he was quirky and odd, and frankly had always had a low opinion of him. He had never before questioned the cost of anything. He had always had money - not a fortune, but enough never to have to worry about cab fares and never needing his wife to go out to work. But the bank had pointed out his deficiencies clearly, without sympathy and frankly in a disparaging way. The bank was right. Anthony had never really taken the whole affair seriously.

There had always been money coming into the firm, and in years past the interest the bank paid for the capital monies held by them was of itself a secure and comfortable income, used to top up office coffers in the lean months. But with the low interest rates this income was no longer there. It hadn't been replaced by anything. All the old-established clients had also become fewer. Where were they? he thought. Were they dead? No, he realised that many of them had retired, and the new brooms coming in had a different approach to legal services. They went online, thought Anthony, to find a lawyer, and didn't necessarily want to go to their family's lawyer or the company's trusted adviser. They looked for the cheapest option. People were ringing around for quotes, weighing up the various conversations with various lawyers, and deciding which one to choose rather than going with the traditional one. Of course, companies all had reduced legal budgets and were obliged to get quotes by their boards. Individuals no longer had any loyalty. There were tie-ups between lawyers and estate agents. Conveyor-belt conveyancing. Tick box mentality. Everything done on the cheap. Rows of licensed conveyancers and executives doing the jobs previously done by solicitors, but at a fraction of the cost. If there was negligence the insurance policy was there to settle it. No wonder insurance premiums had escalated out of all proportion. Why, thought Anthony, had he not seen this coming? He had responsibility for the firm and had to assume responsibility for the mess. He initially blamed his partners for persuading him to take on more IT people and staff, expensive web sites and IT systems. He tried to make himself believe that the problems would not have arisen if he had stuck to his guns and said no. But actually he had got lost in a new world and did not like to admit he had been left behind.

The cab stopped outside the station and Anthony got out. "Twelve pounds please, sir," the driver said. Anthony handed him £15 and walked away. He realised how easily money changed hands. He walked to the barriers, picking up the free paper along the way, as he did every evening, and headed for his train. He climbed on board and made his way down the aisles. Already full. Finding a seat would be tricky. He made for the 'quiet coach' so that he wouldn't have to speak to anyone and would not be interrupted by inane mobile phone users. He wanted peace to reflect.

The departure time came and went. Everyone on the train eager to get home, tired with the day. Over the Tannoy system the message came: "We apologise for the delay to your service. This is due to signalling problems further up the line. As soon as we have more information we will let you know the expected time of departure."

The train remained in the station, doors closed, air conditioning on in most carriages, save for two where it had failed and the travellers in these getting hotter and hotter by the minute. For some reason, though, they stuck it out. On a commuter train no-one really liked to make a fuss at first: resigned acceptance of years of commuting and experiencing everything that could possibly go wrong. Best faced with fortitude and resilience and the vague hope that the 'delay repay' scheme would give you vouchers to redeem against the next season ticket. Commuters accepted anything that could reduce the extortionate cost.

After fifteen minutes the train set off slowly and furtively, as if testing the water. The Tannoy system started: "We again apologise for the delay to your service and the inconvenience caused. The route will now be via the slower line due to problems on the line ahead." Everybody knew that this meant an extra fifteen minutes on the journey in any event. The collective sighing of all the commuters could have been measured on the Richter scale.

"Mind your legs," boomed the girl with the trolley, ramming it into one of the seats, hitting someone's elbow and running over a foot which had had the audacity to be splayed out into the aisle. It then proceeded to get caught up in the long handle of a bag sitting on the floor in front of its owner. Without giving its owner a chance it was off down the aisle with the trolley, only stopping when the trolley hit a suitcase blocking the aisle. Bag retrieved, its owner marched back to her seat and examined the damage.

"You can't leave your case there," the trolley lady said. "You're blocking the aisle. The guard said at the start of the journey that all bags and cases must be stored in the overhead compartment or in the baggage area at the end of the carriage."

The embarrassed owner of the case, a young lady, got up, all eyes on her, and tried to lift the case. She attempted to lift the case into the overhead area, but struggled. The gentleman sitting next to her offered to help, and together the pair manoeuvred the case above their heads. At this point it looked as though it would tip over and into the trolley. The image of small bottles of wine, spirits, crisps and biscuits thrown over the carriage caused amusement to the people round about. Only the day-trippers stopped the trolley to buy things. The commuters knew that it was a habit best avoided, otherwise the cumulative cost would soon outweigh any advantage of the bag of crisps or the chocolate bar. It was like the morning coffee. A regular habit was like buying another season ticket.

Anthony found a seat in the Quiet Coach, not before spotting Eleanor, Simon and Gerry not far away. None of them looked up, fortunately. He sat down in the seat and opened up his free newspaper. But he didn't read it. He went through the motions. He felt numb. He didn't know what to do. He didn't understand how the firm had got to this point and was unable to formulate a plan. He wasn't able to plan as far ahead as tonight. Should he tell his wife? She had never known anything else. She had been born into the office through her father and now married into it through Anthony. She never questioned its existence. It was a fact of life for her. She never had anything to do with it, of course. 'Men's work,' she would say to the ladies who lunched with her. As long as there was an income from it she was not interested in how that income was made. She had never worked and had no intention of doing so. "No," thought Anthony, "I can't tell her." He couldn't tell anyone. He was in reality too ashamed. He was responsible for an office full of staff who had children and mortgages, debts and responsibilities. He was responsible himself for a mortgage and a bank loan and a wife. What could happen, he thought. The bank will call in the loan and the mortgage and the house will go and the wife will go out with the bathwater.

"We apologise for the slow running of your train this evening. This has been caused by signal failure ahead of us" the Tannoy hurtled out. The train came to a stop. It was dark outside and there was no way of knowing where the train was on its journey. "Will the train guard please contact the driver," the Tannoy shouted again. Fifteen minutes passed the train stationary. Thirty minutes passed.

Simon was staring at his computer. He didn't know why. It was a habit. But he wasn't looking at the screen. His eyes were looking through the screen into the depths of depression. He was thinking over the day. He could not believe it had happened. He felt it must be a dream and he would soon wake up. What did they mean, 'redundant'? He had always worked there. He had never been anywhere else. The company couldn't manage without him. He knew it inside out. There must have been a mistake. He fiddled in his pocket and pulled out his letter. The Chairman hadn't even had the decency to give him a heads-up. After all these years, the Chairman's eyes had been turned by the new graduate recruits with their trendy ideas and fancy qualifications. What did they know? All theory, thought Simon. They'll come a cropper. He then had a vicious thought: "And I hope they do," he said to himself. Simon had never wished ill on anyone. He always saw the best in people and situations, which is why he had got on.

"Experience matters," he remembered his Dad saying. Not any more apparently. Simon didn't know what to do. He hadn't looked at the jobs pages since he was sixteen years old. He didn't have a CV. He wouldn't know where to start. He knew there wasn't much to put in it in any event. Who is interested in Beckwith Comprehensive and five 'O' levels, anyway, he thought. What would his Dad have done, he wondered. Sadly, his Dad was no longer around to give advice. But Simon started to question his advice in any case, something he had never done before. He had now lost faith in the two men who had been the biggest influence in his life.

His wife, what would she say? He felt his whole being had been shattered. Every piece of him was reeling. He *was* the company. He had obtained his reason for being from the company. If that was taken away from him he would be nothing. A nobody.

The train started off at a gingerly pace. It immediately juddered to a halt. "We apologise for the delay to your service and the inconvenience caused to you. This is due to signal failure and overhead cable theft. As soon as we have more information we shall pass it on." The Tannoy in full swing.

People started to get up and go to the buffet bar. Blow the expense and the real or imaginary need for that can of lager or coke. The carriage was cooling. It was eerily quiet. Some people were using their mobile phones to explain to their families that they would be late. A girl explained in detail to a friend to "start without her". She then proceeded to tell her friend on the line exactly what she wanted to order at the restaurant. "You get going on the starter and I'll be there as soon as possible," she said down the phone and to the whole carriage.

People grew tense. Patience was tested. Papers discarded on the floor were picked up and read again. It was quiet: no engine noise and no noise from outside; no movement on the track in either direction. "We are in a queue of trains waiting to go through the affected area," the Tannoy boomed out. "We are unable at this stage to give any indication as to the expected time of arrival." The train started to move. For a few minutes it eased forward, and then stopped.

Eleanor was doing the crossword. She hadn't had time in the morning to look at it, as she had been busy preparing her reports. She tried to be optimistic. She still had a job and she knew that many in the bank had been made redundant. She just felt let down, unappreciated for all the long hours she had put in over the years. She knew that the bank felt that she wasn't up to the job. She had failed the test. She was being sent back to the team, to be one of a group. Going solo had been a disaster. She knew it had. She got too involved with the customers' lives. She was always looking to justify her decisions with graphs and statistics. But she knew deep down that no number of figures could help some of her customers. Like her, they were failures, unable to cope in this turgid, difficult, foggy life, where the goalposts kept changing and money got tighter and more expensive. How had it happened? Gradually, she thought, without anyone noticing. Something had changed within her during the few years she had been looking after her father. She had seen raw emotion and physical need. She had dealt with the challenge effectively and efficiently whilst still working full-time. But still the picture of her father slowly deteriorating, sitting in a wheel chair, or lying on a hospital bed, stayed with her. Helpless and hopeless. He was on the "pathway to death", the hospital had told her. Dealing strategically and sympathetically with the end of life, and free car parking at the hospital. A sticker will be provided, they had told her. She remembered the nurse just doing her job and ticking the boxes literally whilst her father lay unconscious on the bed, a sheet barely covering him and in a nappy. Total role reversal and back to basics. Every time she thought about it her eyes welled up with tears. Where was that go-getter who had joined the bank fresh from university? Where had the time gone? Why hadn't she found a husband or had a family? She didn't even have a cat. No time, never at home, she thought.

The train started up again, this time gathering speed. The mood of the carriage changed. People began to busy themselves, collecting their belongings and getting ready to get off. The carriage suddenly felt warmer and more optimistic. The train was on a roll. Nothing was going to stop it.

A screech of brakes, a shuddering of the whole train, crackling and breaking of something underneath. Then stillness and quiet. In the middle of nowhere. Black outside. People started to whisper, "A jumper, a jumper." Commuters knew the signs. Had heard it all before.

"We apologise for the continued delay to your service," the Tannoy shouted out. "As soon as we have any more information we will let you know."

A guard hurried through the carriage to the front of the train.

"Caution, train crew. Disabled alarm activated. Caution, train crew. Disabled alarm activated." The Tannoy changed tack and the level of anxiety increased.

No one looked up. The commuters knew. Another hour at least of delay on a cold, weary train taking cold, weary and tired commuters home after yet another day in the office. The day-trippers became annoyed, marching down to the buffet bar to complain, expecting someone to do something, but only setting themselves up for a fall. No-one could do anything. The police would be called to the scene and the driver would be taken off.

"We apologise for the continued delay to your service. The train guard is investigating the situation and an up-to-date report will be given as soon as possible. If you would like to make your way to the buffet bar, a complimentary tea or coffee or bottle of water will be made available to you."

The trippers rushed to the buffet bar to grab their freebie, unaware of the impact the current delay would have on their journey. The regulars knew. The Tannoy was working overtime tonight. It would shortly run out of excuses and one-liners and have to give them some real lines. Some harsh truth.

Gerry was oblivious to it all. He had been on too many trains, seen too many trains and looked at too many timetables to be fazed, worried or inconvenienced by anything. He remained in his seat, headphones in, trying to cut himself off from the outside world. Of course, this is what he had been doing all his life: cutting himself off, from his wife, his family and now from his job. His life had always been one of routine. He liked routine, which is why he liked timetables. He knew that his wife had found him boring. She had said so in the divorce petition: one of the grounds of unreasonable behaviour. He had shrugged and accepted it when his wife had left him for the local butcher, who seemed to be the antithesis of Gerry. He was a go-getting local businessman who learnt Spanish in his spare time and invented speciality sausages and took holidays to the Iberian peninsula. Gerry had never bothered to ask his wife exactly where that was, but he suspected it was somewhere hot and continental. He fleetingly wondered if you could get there by train, and was determined that he would never let his wife get her hands on his cheap train travel vouchers from work.

"We are being held here awaiting the British Transport Police," the Tannoy started up. "There has been a fatality on the line and the police are required to investigate. The driver is being taken off the train. We apologise for the delay to your service and any inconvenience caused to you. As soon as we have more information we will update you. In the meantime, the guard will be passing through the train to provide connection details." The Tannoy faded out and left the travellers staring in front of them. Impossible to answer, question or sympathise. The Tannoy wasn't a real person, merely a relayer of information, a puppet of the train guard. The commuters knew what this all meant. Sitting in the cold miserable carriage, total quietness descending, picking up the mood of the people who for a period of time were sharing the space, breathing the same air and sharing the expectations of travelling somewhere. Home, a night out, a meal at a restaurant, trip to see friends or relations. It didn't matter what. Everyone was equal, even those in First Class. Very soon all the food, whether complimentary in First Class or for sale in Standard would be gone. No more teas or coffees given away. Fortitude, tolerance and patience would be needed. The Transport Police would investigate and the train would be shunted back to the nearest station. Back to the capital and starting the journey all over again. The driver taken off in need of support, and the train cleaned up. A relief driver had to be found and authorisation from the police to get on the move.

The emergency supplies of hot and cold drinks didn't last very long: small cups and bottles, mini-sized, kept in a cupboard for such eventualities. Travellers fell into two groups: the regulars who had been here before and ignored all the announcements, and the trippers, eager to take up all the offers and soak up the excitement. But even *they* started to look pale after an hour of sitting on the train going nowhere. All the newspapers read, all the crosswords completed IPod music on its sixth round. It grew cold. People started to complain. Quietly at first, to each other, a slow grumble to their fellow-passengers, then on their mobiles to their friends. But then batteries ran out. Imprisoned in a tin carriage going nowhere with nothing left to do.

The Tannoy started up, sensing this growing unease. "The train guard will be passing through the train, handing out the delay repay forms for you to complete. Please feel free to make a claim. We apologise for the inconvenience caused to you." But the claim forms ran out after two carriages. The Tannoy assisted: "Full details can be found on our website."

No food left at the buffet bar or drinks. It grew cold and threatening. Some of the more argumentative travellers began to walk up and down, looking for a train guard. Perhaps wisely, the train guard remained hidden. Then movement. Activity on the line. The police arrived. The driver removed. Lights set up on the track, but still the train remained stationary. Depression set in, desolation and the realisation that no-one had any control over events, the action of a jumper impacting upon a group who would never again be together once their journey had eventually ended - save for the commuters who would have to do the same journey again the next day. Their resignation that this was all part of their lives. The unpredictability of train travel.

Anthony had experienced a number of jumpers in his time. He usually wondered what had led them to such a decision. In fact, he had usually thought they were losers with no backbone, and berated the inconvenience caused to him. He had been unable and unwilling to get into a jumper's mind to understand the pain and suffering. But this time Anthony felt he half-understood. A way out, he thought. The coward's way out or the brave person's way out? He sat in his seat, staring out of the window, looking at his reflection and the reflections of all the other travellers. All the jumper's problems gone, he thought. No more worries or cares. No more bank loans or staff expecting their salaries. No more wife wanting a new car or dress or hundredth pair of shoes.

Simon looked over to Anthony. "Typical, Anthony, isn't it? You've had a bad day and just want to get home and this happens," he said.

Anthony was in no mood for talking, especially to Simon, who always seemed to be on the crest of a wave and having a lucky life. "We've seen it all before, haven't we, Simon?" he replied. "I wish they'd serve up some free whisky. It might make it a bit more manageable."

Simon agreed with Anthony, but Anthony guessed that Simon wasn't a whisky-drinking man, more a half-a-lager man on a Friday night.

"I suppose it's back into the capital and onto another line," continued Simon. "I dread to think what the station is like back there - trains backed up, unable to move."

"Bedlam, I should think," said Anthony, not looking at Simon, but continuing to look into the darkness.

Simon looked back at his computer. He didn't know why, but there was nothing else to do and he liked to be busy. Not that that had helped him, he thought. He realised that he had had enough of doing the expected, behaving in the expected manner, taken for granted. He knew that it was expected that he would just take the redundancy and not cause trouble.

The train was very cold now. No more chatter. The Tannoy started up again. "We shall be returning to the station where you will be transferred to another train." It echoed throughout the carriage.

At least, thought Simon, this was something positive, even though it was in the opposite direction. The train slowly moved backwards and transported its load back to base. It gathered momentum and felt positive. The day-trippers were on an adventure. Something to tell their mates. The commuters were resigned to getting home late again and going to bed, to start the journey again the next day.

They arrived back at the station and were quickly given priority to board a waiting train. There was a stampede, as if it was a race for the best seat. The commuters gradually collected their belongings and trudged off one train and on to another. This was the drill. Done it before. The only advantage was a new carriage with a new set of fellow-travellers. Gerry, Eleanor, Simon and Anthony found themselves at the back of the queue, amongst the last to get on the new train. Others couldn't understand why they were not rushing to find a good seat. They each had a look of resignation and detachment. None of them had their usual jovial chat or witty one-liners. None seemed particularly keen to talk. Thrown together due to circumstances. Each alone in a crowd of travellers, finding seats together in the foreign environment of another train.

The Tannoy started up, this time chirpy and bright, offering special deals on coffee and muffins, wine and crisps. Some took up the offer. Many didn't. They were already over two hours late and would be arriving home ready for bed.

"How long have we been doing this?" Simon said to the other three.

"Too long," said Gerry, who appeared to have lost interest in his Ipod and seemed to want to talk. "Perhaps we should call it a day and do something else," he said.

"But what?" asked Eleanor. "What are we fit for? Not normal jobs in our local town. We would never fit in. We've been away too long."

"No money, either," said Simon. "How can you live," he continued, "on a local salary in a market town?"

"You have to cut your cloth accordingly," piped up Anthony, who, they all thought, had nodded off again against the window, his tie by now crooked and shirt collar looking grubby and damp. "That is the problem," he continued. "We are all obsessed with money. Getting it, spending it. We never have enough. Always want more. Never satisfied."

"I suppose you're right," replied Eleanor, "but how would we be if banks stopped lending and people stopped borrowing to fund their Utopias?"

"What Utopias?" asked Anthony. "Is there ever a Utopia?" he enquired. "*We* need to make do and stop striving for something unattainable. *We* should be satisfied with our lot and reject all this change and eagerness for more."

This was the most that any of them had heard him say in ages. They were all taken aback.

"Look at it this way," continued Anthony. "Are any of us really happy? Are any of us really satisfied with what we have and what we put ourselves through to get it? We've been coerced into thinking that there is something better, and have nearly killed ourselves trying to achieve it," he said.

"Don't talk about killing ourselves," chipped in Gerry, "after what we've just heard. Why do they jump in front of a commuter train at rush hour and inconvenience us all?" he asked.

"Because they are sad," replied Eleanor. "Something has gone wrong in their lives and they don't know how to deal with it. What would you do if you had a problem and didn't know what to do?" she asked.

They all looked at each other and looked blank. No-one answered. It went quiet. The carriage was quiet. The train was speeding along, passing small stations and the place where someone had jumped. No one noticed. No one remembered. Everyone in their own bubble. A moment in time, an inconvenience. A reason for the completion of the delay repay form. Twenty pounds off the next ticket, and someone still picking up the pieces off the railway line in the dark, and someone somewhere weeping.

Anthony leant against the window, pretending to be asleep. Simon looked at his computer, but didn't see anything. Gerry listened to the same round of music for the tenth time. Eleanor tried to get 4 Across, but knew she never would. The train began to slow down as it entered the station and the commuters started yet again to gather together their belongings. Gerry went to get his bicycle from the luggage rack at the end of the carriage, and put on his fluorescent jacket and cycle helmet. Eleanor reached up for her coat, which had been neatly folded and placed inside out on the luggage rack above the seat. She pulled on her kid leather gloves and put on her matching hat. Ready for the night air. Simon managed to pull himself out of the blank stare at the computer, and quickly flicked it shut and put it back into the case. Anthony still leant against the window, snoring slightly.

"Come on, Anthony," shouted Simon. "Wake up. We're here." He touched Anthony on the shoulder and Anthony stirred. He looked grey and very old.

"Oh, right. Are we here?" he asked.

"Yes, come on," called Simon. Anthony quickly pulled himself together, grabbed his briefcase and shuffled to the exit.

All four got off the train and walked towards the station exit. Gerry quickly brought his bike into action. As if by magic, the square, parcel-looking object became a vehicle to get him home, at speed. He jumped on to it and waved to his fellow travellers. "See you tomorrow," he shouted.

"Not if we see you first," joked Simon. They all smiled and Gerry was away into the night, his jacket shining under the streetlights.

Eleanor began her walk home. "Do you want a lift?" asked Simon. "It's late," he added.

"No thanks," replied Eleanor. "I'm only down the road, as you know. The walk will clear my head. Thanks, anyway."

Simon remembered the time when Eleanor had accepted a lift. He had had a small jeep at the time and she had struggled to climb into the front seat. It was too high and she had on a straight skirt and high heels. The combination meant a skirt riding too high for comfort, a slight showing of stocking-tops and heels getting stuck in the steps up to the front seat. Simon smiled to himself. Why, he wondered, did he think about that now? Too many years travelling, he thought. Too many memories. To know people but not know them. To spend a short spell with them every day for years and years. An intimacy, but then again, not an intimate relationship. He walked to his car, a 4x4. He had treated himself last year to a small sports car with his bonus. His wife had been surprised and joked about it. "You're normally so practical. A 4x4 type to cover the country roads to the station." He had let her have the sports car. She had laughed, but then kissed him. He liked to surprise her sometimes. This news was going to be a big surprise. Simon sat in the car and waited. He didn't know why. Perhaps he didn't know how to face her or what to say. Deep down he knew it would be all right. She would brush it off and plan their future. He smiled to himself, put the key in the ignition and started up. He pulled swiftly into the road and waved to Eleanor who was halfway home, walking alone along the dimly lit street.

Anthony slowly walked to his car and got in. An old Jaguar. Still looking good, he thought. A sign of establishment and success. But it was a 1990 version.

A sign of success in 1990. Yes, he thought, the firm was doing well then. Money coming into office account, regular payouts to the partners. Good monthly drawings. His wife had enjoyed it all. But then she had always lived like that. Her father had been at the firm in the good times when solicitors were always busy, respectable pillars of society. When affording school fees, a big house, car and foreign holidays was taken for granted. No-one would have thought it could change. But slowly and imperceptibly it had changed. The public's view of solicitors was poor. They were at the bottom of the food chain. The public thought lawyers were all well-paid and arrogant. They did not realise that, save for a small percentage of lawyers in the top firms, the rest were struggling to make any money at all, and what money they did make went back to pay off the overdraft and keep it at an acceptable level.

Anthony thought back to the meeting at the bank: the humiliation, the surprise. He opened the car door and sat down. He didn't want to go home. He didn't know how to explain everything. He didn't think he could, or indeed he would. His wife could not understand. She would just expect him to go back and sort it out. But he didn't know how to. He looked in the mirror and saw an old, tired, grey face looking back at him. It grew cold and quiet. Everyone who had got off the train had gone home. There was no-one about. He looked at his watch. Nine o'clock. He was tired and hungry and lonely. He started to cry. Big tears fell down his face. He couldn't stop. He got his briefcase off the front seat and got out of the car. He locked it and put the keys in his pocket. He walked back to the station. The 9.12 to the capital was due in. It was on time.

It would be so easy. Just a step off the platform. Guaranteed, finished. Problems solved. He was the dependable type, always someone to sort everything out. No problem too great. But no-one had suspected that he had problems. Everyone - friends, family, work colleagues, took it for granted that he was in control. He was, and in that controlled manner he solved the biggest problem of all. He walked to the end of the platform and stepped out, holding his briefcase as the 9.12 slid into the station. The few people on board heard a crackling underneath the train and the train came to a sudden halt.

Here we go again, again!

"Morning, morning," Simon greeted fellow-travellers as they waited on the platform for the 7.49. "Late again, as usual."

He saw Gerry appear, out of breath and red in the face, attempting as ever to collapse his collapsible bike in readiness for boarding the train.

"Good job it's late again," replied Gerry, "otherwise I would really have missed it this morning."

He said this every morning, thought Simon. I wonder what he would do if the train was ever actually on time, he thought. Then Eleanor walked onto the platform looking elegant, confident and classy as ever. "It's late, Eleanor, as usual," said Simon. "No need to worry." All three looked tired after their late night caused by the delayed train and jumper the night before, and their standard early morning start.

"I wonder where Anthony is. Probably still asleep. He did look shattered last night. If I'd left him," joked Simon, "he'd be in Edinburgh now. No doubt he decided to have a lie-in and get the later train. He's normally here first on the platform, so he must still be in bed."

"I must admit," replied Eleanor, "I did think about it myself, but I woke up at my normal time so I decided to get up as usual."

"Me, too," chipped in Gerry, who had managed to fold up his bike and was keeping it well away from Eleanor's skirt and legs. He wiped away the perspiration about to drip into his eye and decided to remove his helmet there and then rather than wait until he was on the train.

"Goodness," said Simon, "it really *is* late this morning." The board showed it delayed ten minutes. "I wonder what the excuse is this morning," he said. "Leaves on the line, driver not turned up for work, signal failure or theft of overhead wires? Which is it to be this time?" He laughed.

The guard walked along the platform getting ready to greet the train, and then the Tannoy sounded. "We apologise for the late arrival of your train this morning. This has been due to a fatality on the line."

"Oh no," said Eleanor. "Surely that one last night hasn't caused back-ups this morning. I thought they would have had it sorted by now. I don't know that I can face more delays this morning."

"Haven't you heard?" chipped in the guard. "We had a fatality here last night, threw himself in front of the 9.12 Stupid idiot! Nothing left of him, of course. The police have been here all night. Only thing left was his briefcase," he said, shaking his head.

The train arrived and everyone clambered on. Simon, Eleanor and Gerry had to sit together at a table as their normal seats were already taken. The train was busier than usual.

"Why so many people?" Simon asked the train guard.

"Several early morning cancellations due to a fatality last night. Three train loads on one train. Should be fun in half an hour at the next stop. Only room left will be on the roof." He laughed.

Simon, Gerry and Eleanor were pleased to have found seats. They tried to go through their normal routines but it was difficult to adapt to a new seat. Not so much room at a table and close physical proximity to the others meant a forced friendliness. No room to manoeuvre the laptop open without upsetting the face makeup Eleanor had placed on the table in front of her.

"Sorry for this," she said to the others, "but I normally do this in the privacy of my own seat. I hope you don't mind."

The guard came up, checking tickets. "You don't need that, love. You're pretty enough without it." This particular guard always said this to her when he was on this train and Eleanor always smiled at him.

Gerry was struggling to get his fluorescent jacket onto the overhead rack. It smelt of sweat. He then sat down next to Eleanor, who moved slightly further towards the window. Gerry was careful to avoid contact; even though the bike was stored away in the luggage rack at the end of the carriage, he still felt frightened about getting oil on her. The only danger at the moment, though, was dripping sweat on her. "No room left for Anthony now," he said. "He must be on the later one, the bugger. Perhaps I should be. After yesterday I didn't think I would be on this train again."

"Why's that?" enquired Simon. "Did you have a bad day?"

"Yes, not half," Gerry replied. "Privatisation and early retirement," he continued. "I was told yesterday. Been in the job too long and time to go. I've got a meeting with HR this morning. I wasn't going to bother going in, but after a good night's sleep I thought I might as well. See what they are going to offer me. I've not got anyone to look after anymore and most of my mates have already retired. This morning when I woke up it all seemed clearer. I've given all my life to work, and now I'm bloody well going to screw as much as I can out of the bastards. I suddenly thought perks, lots of perks. The perks of retirement. I'll get free rail travel forever. I'll do the trips I've only ever planned in my head and written into time-tables for other people. It'll be like putting two fingers up to them. I'll be able to check out all the European rail companies and their timetables. It's amazing how different everything looks after a good night's sleep, isn't it?" Gerry looked happy and hopeful and eager to tell his fellow-travellers all about his plans. He had no one else to tell. But he was actually excited. At last he could see something other than work. He had been given an opportunity.

"Absolutely," said Simon. "You know, I had a bad day yesterday as well. I've been with my company all my life. I started straight from school. I gave my all to it. Yesterday we were told that it was being taken over by one of its major competitors. Every one of us in the meeting was given an envelope setting out our individual circumstances and a time to discuss them with the Chairman. I was too upset to read my letter properly. As soon as I got to the words that I was being made redundant, I pushed it in my pocket and walked out. I felt entirely lost, as I have never had another job in my life."

"What dreadful treatment," said Eleanor. "How can they do that?" she asked.

"That's how I felt," replied Simon, "at first. I felt let down and frankly frightened. I walked around for ages before getting on the train home. After that awful journey I was so shattered. I fell through the door and told my wife everything. It just ran out of my mouth. To be honest, I don't think I stopped talking for over an hour. The kids were in bed, so it didn't matter. My wife had made an enormous spaghetti Bolognese, my favourite. Through the strands of spaghetti I talked and talked and talked. When I had finished, my wife said to me, 'So what's in the envelope?' To be honest, I didn't know. I hadn't even read it through to the end. I pulled it out of my pocket. It was all crumpled and the paper was soft and old. I opened it up and couldn't believe my eyes. I read it out to my wife. 'Wow,' she said, 'with a lump sum like that we can do anything. Start afresh. Do something different with our lives. Give up all that commuting and see the kids grow up."

Simon smiled. "I'd never thought to read the letter to the end. I was too upset and disillusioned with the people I had worked with. But I then realised that I'd never given myself an opportunity to think about an alternative life. I had just accepted the lifestyle I was living without question. This lump sum makes me able to take an opportunity for a different life, one where I can see the kids during the day and not just through a dark room. Do you know, I used to pop into their bedrooms every night when I got home? They would always be fast asleep and I just looked at them, reminding myself of what they looked like. I did the same in the morning as I left the house at dawn, leaving my wife asleep in bed, getting dressed by the light of the en-suite, quietly closing the front door. Everyone in the house and in the street fast asleep and me going to work. To be honest, I never questioned it. Now I realise the stupidity of it. I'm taking the money and making a change. I want to see my family grow up and be a full-time Dad, not a weekend Dad. I want to go to parents' evenings and school concerts. I want to wake up with my wife, not leave her sleeping. It took a shock for me to realise this. Of course, the money helps." He laughed.

"Too right," said Eleanor. "Money always gives you choices. That's what it's all about, isn't it?" She looked at Simon and Gerry, her make-up half-done, one eye with eyeshadow on and one without. She didn't seem to care. "My job has been giving people those choices. Do you know, I've been dealing with small business loans for the last year, dealing with individuals trying to keep their businesses afloat, to beat off the competition and expand into different markets - to keep going, basically. It's tough out there. When there's no money, all choices stop. Nowhere to go, unable to do anything. The inability to effect change. My loans enabled people to achieve their goals and survive. Unfortunately, a number of people didn't survive. The market out there was too tough for them. My area manager said I was too soft on them, gave them too much leeway, extended their overdrafts and repayment periods on loans. But this just got them into even bigger messes. But you know, I saw the person behind the business. For the first time, this year I realised that it wasn't just about figures and graphs; it was about people," she said, with an open, wide expression on her face, as if she had made a huge discovery.

"I bet that went down a bundle with your Area Manager," joked Simon. "Not the sort of talk he wants. It's all just figures for the likes of them." Simon knew full well the pressures that Eleanor was talking about.

"You're right," she replied. "He demoted me. Yesterday, actually. He told me that being the Business Accounts Manager had not worked out, and so he was sending me back to Head Office to work in the team - planning, figures and graphs. Everything I am used to and all I wanted for years. But, you know, I've seen the other side of the figures and statistics. I see now what they really represent: thousands of individuals with their own lives and their own stories. I've given my all to the bank. Like you, Simon, I've sold myself to the bank as you did to your company. The only difference," she said, laughing, "is that they're not giving me a whopping big lump sum, just a demotion. Money gives choices, you see. I don't have a choice."

"Yes, you do," said Gerry. "Pack in, do something else. You'll have built up a good pension after all those years in the bank. Cash it in. Opt out. Don't be abused by them. Tell them to stuff their job up their arses and get out," he quipped.

"But what could I do?" asked Eleanor. "I'm fifty-eight years old. Never had time to get married or have kids. I haven't even had a cat." She laughed. "I just thought when I woke up this morning that I would just carry on as usual, to be pushed around." She had now done both eyes and was starting to look normal and not straight out of a fright show. All she needed was the mascara to finish the job off and present her usual business face to match her business suit.

"Rubbish," said Gerry. "Pack in. Come with me to Europe on the train. Have an adventure. I wouldn't make you ride a bike but you'd have to get into civvy clothes. Throw away the shirts and suits." He looked alive and enthusiastic as if they were already on that adventure.

Eleanor looked at him and Gerry looked at her. What had he said? Whoops, he thought, put my foot in it good and proper. He had never spoken so much in his life, especially to a woman. He was normally too scared of them and kept his distance. He didn't know why he had spoken to Eleanor in this way. Perhaps, he thought, because when he had woken up he did feel different. Liberated, freed from his routine. A chance to be different.

Eleanor smiled. She had never opened up so much in her life and frankly had rarely been so close, either physically or mentally, to a man. Revealing her inner thoughts had never come easy. It had just spilled out this morning. She felt a closeness to Gerry and Simon, something she had not experienced before.

"Gerry's right," Simon said to Eleanor enthusiastically. "Take him on. Have a trip together. At least you're chums. You're both used to travelling long distances on the train, after all. Take one to Paris or Berlin for a change. Gerry's right, Eleanor. Have an adventure. You might have fun. Even if you don't, you can come home and there would be no need to see each other again."

"I might just take you up on that offer, Gerry," she said.

"Well, no time like the present, Eleanor," he said to her. "I shall be away at the end of the week, so don't take long with your decision-making." Gerry laughed. He never thought he would be asking a woman to join him on a trip. He still couldn't believe that he had in fact invited her. Couldn't believe that he had actually said the words. He thought back to the oil marks on her legs way back, and the look she had given him. It was a different Eleanor looking at him now. She seemed softer. Maybe it was the light or the fact that he had seen her close up, before the make-up had gone on: the real Eleanor under the lipstick and eyeshadow, the vulnerable Eleanor.

The train sped along, all seats taken, travellers standing in the aisles and in the 'vestibules' at the end of each carriage. Trying to read papers or books, balancing laptops and Kindles, trying to make some private space where none existed. The countryside merged into a grey-green. Grey sky, green trees, water lying on the ground. The carriage full of gentle murmurings, quiet conversations, people in their own worlds, doing their own things: reading, listening to music, papers balanced on knees, occasionally falling on the floor under the seat opposite, a retrieval by foot, the trolley coming by, running over the papers and anything in its path, its driver as ever looking bored and disillusioned. "Teas, coffees, hot drinks," shouted the trolley-girl down the carriage. Too late. Everyone by this time settled, lulled by the gentle movement of the train into a quiet stupor, imprisoned in a metal tube with no escape until the end of the line. A train sped past in the opposite direction, waking up a sleeper leaning against the window. The commuter train. Everyone going to work. The journey undertaken each and every day. The young, the old, the middle-aged, the happy, the sad, the enthusiastic and the disillusioned, all together with a common purpose. Some enjoying the newness of it, the excitement and bustle, some resigned to it after thirty years of travel, waiting to retire. Some scared of what lay ahead at work, some with an adrenalin rush, anxiously reading documents or working on their computers. A group of people from a company, on an away-day trip to Head Office, taking advantage of their expenses with as much coffee, muffins and cakes as they could manage on the hour-long journey, talking about the office and the girls and the Christmas party.

But at the table for Gerry, Eleanor and Simon, it seemed different. They had stopped talking now. They were all just looking forward with a gentle, glazed look in their eyes. Gone was the frantic computer work or spreadsheet checks, gone the headphone music isolation into their own world, occupying a corner small and confined. Instead, they had all opened up to each other, the first time in over fifteen years at least. They had indeed on this particular morning all been on a very long journey to a place they had never been to before. They had arrived at a feeling of contentment, free from anxiety, deadlines, rules and regulations. They all felt liberated, freed both mentally and physically to do something different. They felt in control of themselves for the very first time.

The train slowed down as it approached the capital, the grey sky and green trees giving way to grey roof-tops and concrete houses, blocks of flats, a football ground and a building site. Heavy traffic on the roads, people on platforms waiting for the small local services. The commuters started to fidget, laptops put away, reaching up to collect coats and bags. Scarves and hats being put on. Some started to leave their seats and attempt to walk up to the front of the train to be the first ones out and down into the Tube or onto the streets. Adrenalin pumping, hearts beating, getting ready for the day.

"We are now approaching our final destination. Please remember to take with you all your personal belongings and take care when stepping onto the platform." The Tannoy in action again. "We apologise for the slight delay to your service and any inconvenience caused to you," it continued, bland statements, of course. The rail company was not bothered about the inconvenience, but it had its list of excuses and this was on it.

Simon, Gerry and Eleanor started to come to life. "Well," said Simon, "we'd better get off. We can't stay here all day. We've got our future lives to sort out. I hope Anthony's on tonight. He'll be surprised with our news. Perhaps it will make him think about changes. He certainly looked hacked-off last night. He must be ready to finish. It's amazing what a good night's sleep does for you."

"Too right," said Gerry. "I feel so much better than I did on the train last night. I feel a weight has been lifted off my shoulders. Pity that bugger who threw himself in front of the train last night didn't give himself a good night's sleep. Time to think over things."

"Yes," said Eleanor, "and that person who did the same at our station. I wonder who it was?"

Epilogue

Simon went on to create a business consultancy firm near to where he lived. He paid off his mortgage, and had two more children whom he saw every day of the week in daylight.

Eleanor did go on that adventure with Gerry. She went on a number of adventures with him, the greatest of which was to Berlin, where they got married - the biggest adventure of them all.

Gerry lived out the rest of his life with a big smile on his face. He ditched the bike (Eleanor didn't like the oil)

Anthony's widow had to sell the house after the bank foreclosed on the mortgage. She used all her savings to pay off his debts. She ended up with dementia and in a state care home, never able to accept her husband's suicide. The dementia meant that she had soon forgotten about it.

The briefcase was never collected from lost property.